The Hilltop

(A College Tale)

Rob + Karrie —

Hope you enjoy it!

Michael J. Bellito

MJ Bellito

Strategic Book Publishing and Rights Co.

Strategic Book Publishing and Rights Co., LLC
USA | Singapore
www.sbpra.com

For information about special discounts for bulk purchases, please contact Strategic Book Publishing and Rights Co., LLC. Special Sales, at bookorder@sbpra.net.

ISBN: 978-1-949483-03-1

To Milo James, my cute new grandson

ACKNOWLEDGMENTS

Erin Brooks, my all-time favorite editor

Front Cover Photo by Lisa Lewis,
Mount Vernon, Iowa

Other books by Michael J. Bellito

Ten Again

First Time Around

Abner's Story

The Silent Journey

Contents

Chapter 1 – Home

As we race toward the dying orange glow on the horizon, I realize it will be dark by the time we arrive. We cross the Mississippi; the current moves along so as not to disturb one's solitude. The car's quiet engine is the only noise as it glides past the golden cornfields. The last rays of the sun dance on the tops of the stalks, and the silent rows of corn bow down in anticipation of a cool autumn night. I love the Midwest. The four changing seasons keep the mind and body alert, from hot summer to brisk fall to cold winter to blooming spring. Autumn is my favorite time though. Tonight is the perfect night for the first homecoming.

"It's pitch dark behind us, Sean," says Dennis, his voice coming out of the back seat to break the silence in the small Vega.

"Yeah, it sure is," I remark as I turn my body around in the seat and strain to look out the rear window.

"We'll be there in another hour and a half," chips in Don as he applies more pressure to the accelerator. "It isn't dark yet except at the Big U."

I like the University. It's not as small or scenic as the Hilltop, and surely not as friendly, but it has its good points. One or two, anyway. But I won't miss it this weekend. I can walk up to some freshman who doesn't know me from President Nixon, and he'll still smile and say hi. Trying to encourage someone at the Big U to respond in that fashion is somewhat akin to sprinting up the side of Mt. Rainier. They must have a course at all big universities that teaches noninvolvement: Tunnel Vision 101. The least they could do is offer it to poor graduate students who come from small colleges. But that is the real world.

Tonight I am going home.

We draw closer to the campus with each revolution of the tires and miles away from graduate studies. Whatever tomorrow holds, this time is blessed. This weekend I will see the old buildings, walk the tired paths, breathe the familiar air, and never grow old or get married or have kids or die. This is life. I'm just a college kid, and as long as I pay my room and board and take an occasional test and turn in my papers on time, I can live forever with my friends close by. I can pretend I'm concerned with civil rights one week, and march against the War the next. I can play football all afternoon and read a novel that very same night. Or maybe I can stay out too late and sleep through my eight o'clock class the next morning. The professor can't fire me. I'll quit first. I can always drop his class and pick up an art class. They let kids experiment in college. That's what it's for.

The car twists its way through the curves of Highway 1. No one is talking, but we all know how close we are to wetting our pants. What is it like being away for five months? It has never been more than a leave of absence. Three and a half months every summer. But this is different. It's not the length, but the permanency that matters. Some famous author – damned English courses – once said that you can never go home. Well, we'll see about that.

The headlights cut through the blackness as we bounce rigidly on the cold seats. I love riding in a car, especially shotgun. The death seat. It would be a nice way to die. I don't mean an accident. I could drift away from life riding silently in the still air of the violent machine, lost completely in my thoughts, a prisoner of the speed and the night and the scenery.

"Hey, guys, we're really close now. Next hill we pass over should put us in sight." Don's voice is electric.

As the Vega rises to the top of the hill, I spot the famous Chapel, which sits atop the tallest hill on campus and is seen for miles into the country.

"Hey, there's the Chapel!" I shout.

"We're home!" yells Dennis.

"Look at it," I continue. "Have you ever seen anything so beautiful in your whole life? Just look at it. Boys, we are gonna have a ball tonight."

The sight of the campus lights in the wooded areas surrounding the Chapel drives us into spasms of joy. I roll down the window, stick my head out, and scream, "We're home! Do you hear me, people?"

Some cows in a nearby field gaze at the passing vehicle with the nut hanging out the window.

"Get back in the car," screams Don. "We don't want to lose you now."

"Oh, yes, we do," says Dennis, as he mockingly tries to shove me out the window. The ensuing struggle causes us all to laugh. The car is alive with the sound of freshmen, and not the serious grad students that we are.

The daily concentration devoted to the study of law is already setting permanent ridges under Don's eyes, and his shock of reddish-blond hair is receding at the temples. It's our fourth straight year as roommates, and I have grown to appreciate his almost insatiable appetite for knowledge. He, too, misses the carefree days. Although he always studied longer and harder than the rest of us, it was a small portion of time compared to the hours he now works in his first year of law school.

Dennis, who roomed with me during my freshman year, is studying for a Master's in English at a neighboring university in Illinois. He is feeling the pressure that accompanies preparing for an advanced degree. His thick, black hair and drooping moustache accent his normally sullen countenance, and his battered grey hat is ornamented with a McGovern for President button.

Come to think about it, I have studied more than I ever thought possible as I strive to earn a Master's in Speech. And I've been teaching two classes of university freshmen each semester as well. Who would have thought of that four years ago? No way.

In fact, the changes in all of us have been subtle when measured yearly, but remarkable since that first year when we met each other. Tonight "les boys" are back together again. And there will be more before this night is over. Don and I picked up Dennis as we cut across the heart of Illinois. Others are coming from Missouri, Wisconsin, Minnesota, even Texas. The evening is very much alive as we pull into Pleasant Valley, the quaint Iowa town that harbors the small college.

We roll to a stop outside a friend's house in town. It's not any friend, it's Paul Mathews, a tall kid with a loud laugh who stayed on campus for one more year as a college recruiter. He would drive from here to there all over the Midwest to encourage kids to come to the Hilltop.

He charges out to greet us with the same ole' phrase he always used. "Shit. Shit. Shit. It's all my old friends back on campus. How you doing? Come in and see my abode. It's not much, but it's wonderfully old and beat-up."

We pile into his house, compliment him on his sparse furniture, and question him on who else he's seen.

"No one. But there's a reunion meeting planned for ten o'clock at the Corner." (This was a local bar where students drank beer and ate pizza for uncounted years.)

I quickly tire of Paul's stories about how he's talked nearly one-third of the Midwest into making a commitment to come to the Hilltop. I have to see the campus – how different I feel now as compared to four years ago. As quickly as I have this feeling, I leave the jubilant group with my promise of attendance at the meeting.

I walk out into the cold night air. The October moon beams down on the battered brick streets as I climb slowly toward the lights of the campus. I feel the chill breeze whip my long, brown hair off my ears, and I tug my red and black lumberjack coat closer to my exposed neck.

As I reach the far end of campus and walk past the Chemistry building, I am suddenly hit with déjà vu. I have been here before. Many times. My now shaky legs have crossed this ground hundreds of times. And yet this time it's completely different – like a time machine. I'm a college kid again, and my friends are here. And these old, weak buildings will never crumble.

As I stand in the center of the mall and gaze upward at the brilliant stained-glass Chapel windows, framed by the white stone nearly a century old, my head spins freely. I turn slowly around and look carefully at all the buildings, dorms, and trees. As I spot the remote English building standing in the far corner of the mall, I think about what's-his-name and laugh. You <u>can</u> go home, you big dummy. You really can.

19

Chapter 2 – The Week That Was, But Probably Shouldn't Have Been

My parents and I climbed into their beige Buick. We were all going for a ride. It would change who I was with new friends I hadn't met yet. As per 1968, we were carrying all we would need for a freshman at college. No computer, cell phone, TV, or car. There would be no need to build bunk beds; the room would stay as it was. A couple of suitcases and some hanging clothes; my mom had taught me how to iron. And a nice kit with all the materials I'd need to shower, shave, deodorize, and look reasonably decent. There was a barber downtown; enough said.

I was convinced that I was looking at my parent's faces for the last time. They were actually leaving. They were going home and deserting me to die of either homesickness or overexposure to campus food, whichever came first. And they were smiling. My mom, who cried when my little sister graduated from K-5 school, didn't have a hint of moisture around her eyes. Did they know something I didn't? Were they fighting back inner grief? Were they trying to show me they loved me and knew I would make it? Had they found out the college would foot the bill for my funeral?

"Now you take care and study hard," my dad said.

"Yes, and make sure you get enough rest," chimed in my mom.

As they climbed into their car, my mom added, "And don't eat too many French fries."

That was it. They had gone home. They had left me to grow from a boy to a man, to study hard so I could face the world with some degree of intelligence, to meet other people and learn to accept or at least tolerate different points of view. And their parting words of wisdom were, "Don't eat too many French fries."

I was assigned a dorm room on the fourth floor of Nilo Hall. It was the top floor of the building and had been used for storage space until increased enrollment during recent years had forced the school to open additional rooms. Affectionately referred to as the attic, fourth floor was inhabited almost exclusively by incoming freshmen.

How nice, I thought, as the burly senior helped us upstairs with the luggage. I hadn't yet heard about Monkey March.

Dennis Summers, who sported a crew-cut that first year, shared room 404 with me (Sean McKay); Don Johnson and Ed Barkley, our conservative and liberal opposites, lived next door in 406; Mike Smith, an amiable Iowan, and Paul Mathews, a tall, skinny comedian, occupied room 407; Arnie Elston, a fanatic of the film "The Graduate" (who would repeatedly say, "Katherine Ross is boss"), and Woody Beard, a chess player, shared room 405. The end room, 401, housed Chuck Stanton and Jim Veers, who were destined to spend the entire year fighting off wasp attacks, which originated from their very own built-in nest adjoining the window.

1968 was the one year they did not make the frosh wear purple-colored beanies. I don't know why, and I never did find out. Being on campus did not automatically entitle one to the position of freshmen, which was ranked a full two steps below any wandering mongrel who happened to drift through on a rainy day. One was expected to earn that distinction. There were roughly three stages that had to be successfully accomplished before one was allowed to attend the first day of classes. They were: the President's Reception, Monkey March, and registration. The first two are capitalized, and rightly so. Once they were survived, the third trial was relatively easy.

After two full days on campus, the frosh felt ready to meet President Skanks. He didn't invite us to his house. We had the honor of meeting him in the Union, the common ground for students. (The cafeteria was there, and all dances were held on the orange carpet.) According to custom, we were forcibly paired up with a dream date, whom we were expected to entertain for the entire evening.

Garbed in my dress shirt and pants, a tie, and the only coat I owned, I ambled across the campus. I thought about all the social amenities I had learned in high school. I knew I shouldn't fart, belch, or sneeze loudly, but besides those, I didn't know what to expect. Maybe if I had had a few decent dates while in high school. In a situation such as this, I was an expert at fouling it up by myself.

Whose idea was this, anyway?

I walked up the cracked steps and through the wide doors of Gordon Hall, where the boys were to be matched with the girls. I strolled into the parlor. All the other guys were waiting, looking sharp in their jackets and ties. I stood in a corner, sweating, and waited for the death chime to ring.

It came bustling through the door in the form of Mrs. Chambers, the dorm mother of Gordon Hall, who loudly proclaimed as she swept past us waving her arms, "Come along, gentlemen. The young ladies are waiting. Oh, you are lucky young men. The ladies look charming tonight. So charming. Now, come this way."

We were herded out to the front lobby, where we glanced up to the second floor and saw the bottom half of all the charming young ladies. As Mrs. Chambers lined us up according to height, the nervous giggles of the girls could be heard drifting down from above. I slipped a last Pepto Bismol tablet into my mouth. That made four in the last hour, but my stomach still felt queasy. The girls filed slowly down the wide staircase, the short ones in front.

My stomach took a final flip-flop, and I gasped for a last breath of air. As I looked up and down our silent line, I realized I was not alone in my nervousness.

As they came to a halt, the girls were paired up with their dates one by one. An attractive girl with blue eyes and brown hair stopped next to me. Putting on my biggest smile, I introduced myself to her.

I'll never forget the look of horror that darkened her face as she stared into mine. I strongly suspected she wouldn't enjoy my company once she got to know me, but I didn't expect her to be immediately repulsed.

"Is there anything wrong?" I asked politely.

"Your teeth are pink," she said.

Damned Pepto Bismol. It almost ruined me. After a hasty drink of water, I escorted my date outside and down the winding path toward the Union. Since she was quiet as a corpse, I was forced to attempt small talk.

"I never got your name," I said.

"It's Eunice."

"Oh, that's a lovely name," I lied.

Silence.

"It sure is a nice evening."

No reply.

"Yeah," I continued, "I really like it out here this evening. It's nice and peaceful. I like peace and quiet, don't you?"

She obviously did. We endured our walk in relative silence, with the exception of my stomach, which was making unseemly noises. She glanced once more at the growling noise, and I probed her for light conversation.

"Boy, that sun sure is bright. It's right in our eyes. I can't remember the sun being down so low on the horizon. Can you?"

"It's there every night at this time," she replied curtly.

We finished our walk without a word.

When we arrived at the Union, all the couples, hoping to make a good first impression, lined up to meet President Skanks. It was a very big deal. None of us knew a college president, and we assumed he could expel us instantly if he didn't like us. After all, it was his college. I figured my chances had diminished with Eunice on my arm. I prayed that the president hadn't been popping Pepto Bismol tablets.

The first meeting was a success. The silver-haired gentleman was very kind. His delightful wife told us to visit them in their home anytime. I cringed and waited for Eunice to say something inappropriate. Thankfully, she remained mute. After the initial greeting by his highness, the kids were "free to get to know each other."

Oh, brother. Well, I'd just have to push on and see what would happen next.

I stood with my companion along the rail surrounding the orange carpet, watching the dance floor fill with couples. I cleared my throat. Barely touching her arm, I leaned closer to her and asked, "Eunice, would you care to dance?"

"No, but I would like a Coke." Eunice certainly didn't waste words.

The Cat was a favorite hangout of students. Located on the lower level of the Union, its official name was the Canteen. I guess it was called the Cat for short because it would have been too embarrassing to ring up a girl and ask, "Would you like to go to the Can with me?"

I had stuffed thirty dollars in my wallet so I would be prepared for anything. I wiped the sweat from my palm and pulled my wallet from my back pocket. There wasn't a girl in the world who could remain unmoved by the sight of a wad of money.

That was it. Eunice was smiling. She laughed for the first and only time that evening, and her voice rang out clearly. "I didn't know they still made wallets with zippers. Does that keep your money safe?"

The rest of the evening dragged. I discovered more about Eunice's personality over our drinks. She liked Mike Royko and Winnie the Pooh, hated television and organized religion, and didn't know who the Chicago Cubs were.

I also discovered how long one can suck an ice cube before it dissolves. She soon complained of a headache, and asked to be dismissed.

"May I walk you home?"

"Sure. Why not?"

When we reached the outer door, we were both surprised to see the summer rain pouring down from the night sky. I painfully recalled the setting sun two hours earlier. I slipped off my double-breasted jacket and said, "It is my sincere wish that this coat may keep your beautiful hair pristine."

She once again assumed the pose of a mummy coming back to life for the first time in a thousand years. She was staring at my body. I skimmed my shirt. The dark sweat stains began at both armpits and spread down to about three or four inches above my belt. My eyes locked on the wet blobs. I was humiliated, two-toned variety.

When I looked up again, I saw Eunice and some guy with an umbrella splashing through puddles on their way to her dorm.

****

On the night following the President's Reception, Dennis and I were roused from our sleep at one-thirty by what sounded like a tree being rammed through our door. "C'mon you stupid monks. Get your asses out here. Move it!"

The gentleman at our door was inviting us to come outside for an hour of fun and games, and he wasn't taking no for an answer. This was the second step before we were officially designated as freshmen on campus. The girls had to sing and dance during lunch hour in the Union. The guys had to participate in these recreational activities, which were all grouped under the heading of Monkey March.

The freshmen were, naturally, the "Monkeys." This could have something to do with the religious background of the school, but I doubted it, unless the Inquisition counts.

The Hilltop looked different in the middle of the night. The light from the lamp posts was barely visible through the fog. The misty atmosphere and the cold rain mixed together to give us the feeling that we were part of an Edgar Allan Poe story. And the huge president's house on top of the large hill behind us seemed like the House of Usher.

"All right, you stupid monks, line up," boomed out the thunderous voice of Big Red. The entire time we were directed through calisthenics, Big Red's voice split the night as he barked out orders and insults. He was a typical college jock. His favorite pastimes were playing football, watching football, and drinking himself into a blind stupor on beer. Beer was the only drink for him. A mixed drink required measured proportions and was above his math level.

Big Red was a legend in his own time. He was designated leader by his peers solely on the credit of his remarkable rhetoric. His masterful delivery would have put Plato to shame. His vocabulary would have put Long John Silver to shame.

The most famous tale concerning his behavior had been passed down for three successive years. During his freshman year, Big Red strolled into the TV room to watch the Bears game. The guys were already watching an AFL game on another channel. Big Red stood at the front of the room with an expression of shock on his face and addressed the assembly. "Hey, what's this shit? Let's watch the Bears game!"

Nobody moved. Suddenly, one soul yelled out, "We'd rather watch this game!"

Big Red stared smugly at them and said, "Oh, is that a fact? Well, if we're not watchin' the Monsters of the Midway, then we're not watchin' nothing."

He calmly ripped the plug out of the wall, hoisted the TV up on his massive shoulder, and pitched it through the window. Fact or fiction, it was a most impressive story, the ideal type on which legends are built.

Big Red's beer belly stuck out of his t-shirt, pressed wet by the rain. His red shorts were baggy, and he tugged to keep them up. His right hand grasped a huge wooden paddle, which we prayed would not be used on us.

After our "warm-ups," we were led down the hill to a doorway in the back of the big gymnasium. The dark stairs leading to the fieldhouse were lined with upperclassmen. They all held paddles, and the hollow sound of their chants rang in our ears as we were forced down the steps in pairs. "Beat their buns! Beat their buns!"

The black dungeon awaited us eagerly. Our tennis shoes slopped through the mud, and we shrieked as the cold spray from a garden hose lashed out at our unsuspecting bodies. Laughter filled the dark tomb as we were steered into one corner of the fieldhouse.

Sitting in the mud, most of us got to watch a relay race, in which guys had to run to one end of the track, remove their pants, and come back. The losers of this contest were treated to a scrambled egg surprise - shell included – in the back of their shorts, hand delivered by the winners.

After a few more freshmen were honored in a greased pig chase, our entire squad was taken outside. We were led to the girls' half of the campus. I was to learn later that this was the main event of Monkey March. The frosh sat in a circle on the porches and sang obscene songs for about ten minutes, after which we shouted in unison, "We want rain! We want rain!"

The girls obliged by dumping hot, cold, soapy, and perfumed water on us. This was occasionally spiked with mustard, ketchup, or other spices. The real treat was when they threw down various articles of underclothing as souvenirs.

(Gordon Bowen, a new friend, lost his glasses; they would take two weeks to replace.)

When we finally made it back to our dorms, our clothes stained with mustard, we breathed a sigh of relief over never feeling the weight of one of those paddles being used on us.

Mike Smith suddenly appeared, holding up a rather large size of pink panties. "Long live Monkey March!" he yelled. Well, something for everyone.

****

The day before classes began, we embarked upon our third and final test as incoming students. Registration was held in the large gymnasium where the college basketball games were played. I weaved through the maze of tables, signing up with various departments for courses. At every table, the kindly old lady or the tired gentleman signed us up for the boring introductory course, which was required for all novice students.

I scratched my signature on the only important document as far as the college was concerned, a personal check covering room, board, and tuition fees, and walked out into the sunlight. I took a deep breath of the hot, humid air and sighed heavily. I had just been placed in four courses I hadn't planned on taking and couldn't care less about. Regardless, I felt good inside. I was a college student at last.

Chapter 3 – Is This the Army?

We were up at the crack of dawn. I spent an hour reading <u>before </u>breakfast. The printed word was the king of the college campus. Spoiled by years of television, freshmen were curtly reacquainted with the forgotten art of reading. Everybody studied constantly the first month of school simply to keep our heads above the tide of reading material assigned by college professors. One English prof told us he read whenever he went to the john. If one planned on finishing all the books for his course, the student would have to follow in his footsteps. Twelve books were simply too many. And my checkbook, of course, was empty, courtesy of the college bookstore on the day after registration.

The students usually chose to read as much of each book as possible, until the prof moved on to the next one. Since most college teachers only test with a mid-term (most profs rely on three papers), students have the quarter to try to catch up. I never did, and normally skipped one or two books a quarter, using my street wisdom to determine which were the least important.

****

Rules and regulations. That was the name of the game. Through my entire senior year in high school, I had heard from a million different sources that a person could take any courses he wanted, study if and when he felt like it, and generally choose his own lifestyle when he reached college. Besides the hazing of freshmen that first week and a bombardment of reading material from professors, there was a constant barrage of rules to be learned and followed. I didn't remember enlisting in the military. I must have been drafted.

Most of the rules concerned dormitory policy that strictly curtailed one's social life. There were designated hours during the day for just about everything in the "barracks," and if anyone disobeyed, he was promptly fined. There were quiet hours, which were for study. There were noise hours, which were for noise. The latter encompassed the hours reserved for lunch and dinner meals. It was ironic that these were usually quieter than the quiet hours, because everybody was eating in the Union, and the dorm was deserted. All day Saturday was "noise" day, but nobody made much then either. We were too well-trained.

Girl hours were known as "open dorm." Nilo Hall had open dorm on Sundays from two to five. Three hours once a week, girls were allowed to visit boys in our rooms, provided that the door remained open at all times. This meant that if a guy's mother or grandmother or sister happened to visit on Saturday, they would have to chat in the lounge or walk around campus.

The history of these rules was interwoven with the Methodist affiliation in the founding of the college. Sex of any kind was taboo. The six-foot rule was still in the books, which stated that a boy and a girl could walk together on campus only if they were six feet apart. No one followed this anymore. (The revolution first began back in 1926 when a handful of students danced on campus.)

Most of the outdated rules were still adhered to by everyone on campus, especially the freshmen. A short chain of command existed to make sure there were no deviations. The "sergeants" were the floor proctors, who were usually the worst offenders. To become a proctor, one had to fill out a form which gave the dean of men, who made the final selection, an idea of how each guy would handle various situations. The following were typical questions:

What would you do if you caught a fellow student making noise during quiet hours?

A. Tell him to be quiet.

B. Tell him to be quiet and warn him not to make noise again.

C. Tell him to be quiet and fine him.

D. Fine him. *

What would you do if you caught a fellow student sneaking illegal beverages (beer, liquor, etc.) into his dorm room?

A. Warn him and make him leave the dorm immediately.

B. Confiscate the illegal material.

C. Consume the illegal material and fine him.

D. Fine him. *

What would you do if you caught a fellow student with a member of the opposite sex in his dorm room with his door shut during closed dorm hours?

A. Warn him and tell the girl to leave.

B. Remind him of the hours and break the door off the hinges.

C. Confiscate the girl and fine him.

D. Fine him. *

*All money resulting from fines must be turned in along with any illegal material (booze, girls, etc.) to the office of the dean of men.

If an upperclassman with a sour disposition answered "D" to all of the above questions, he was on the short road to becoming a proctor. He would work in conjunction with his floor partner to uphold the dorm rules by any means possible, including terrorism, extortion, and capital punishment.

Fourth floor Nilo proudly boasted Fred and Mark, whose personalities were as different as night and day. Fred was nice, but he never did his job. He was known as the Phantom Proctor, because he was never in the dorm. He was always out drinking at night. And we were shocked - more than once - by his prostrate body being assisted up the stairs by four of his buddies after a "keggar." He occasionally surprised us when we were too noisy and told us to be quiet. He never fined us. I still don't know how he passed the dean's test.

Mark, who was definitely the night half of the team, carried his power beyond limitations. He would constantly sneak around in tennis shoes in an attempt to catch some poor fool laughing too loud or banging a door. Swooping down on the offender, he would scream some inanity about the law of the land, in this case, the dorm. Mark would always: D. Fine him. *

By the middle of October, Ed Barkley, Don's roommate in 406, informed us that he was going to celebrate reading days with some beer. Reading days consisted of a free three-day weekend once each semester in which students were supposed to catch-up on their reading. Most students chose to go home. Others found ways to commemorate the first Saturday without classes. (Yes, there were Saturday classes!) Don, Paul, and I agreed to go along with Ed's bold scheme to sneak beer into the dorm.

Ed was years ahead of his time or years behind; I could never figure out which it was. Anyway, he was not drumming along with the rest of us. His unfortunate roomie, Don, had to glue his eyelids open in preparation for Ed's late-night blathering on Eastern religion and philosophy. The dark room and soft pillow would seduce Don into sweet dreams hours before Ed finished his monologue on the Lord's Prayer compared with the Om. Ed was the first to try transcendental meditation, the first to inhale marijuana, and the first to invent poetry, or at least improve the technique. His greatest original poem featured two dogs copulating on somebody's front lawn, and his favorite saying was, "It's true. I read it in Ramparts."

Room 406 contained a secret hideaway directly behind the dresser mirror. It was accidentally discovered one night by Ed, who was checking to see if the FBI had bugged his room so they'd get hot tips on the upcoming revolution. Ed assumed that it had been previously used to conceal beer and booze.

Friday night. Ed carried two six-packs of beer under his coat. Don opened the door for him following the secret knock. Grinning eagerly, Ed slid the mirror off the wall revealing the hiding place.

"Shit. Shit. Shit," said Paul. "Did you cut a hole in the wall?"

"No," answered Ed. "I found this last month. Pretty cool, huh? If anyone knocks on our door, we just stick the beer in here, slide the mirror back on, and open the door."

The next hour was spent drinking and laughing over old college stories. Whenever a bunch of guys sit around and drink, they tell old college stories. It's tradition. Having been at school for a month and a half, we were seasoned veterans at last. As we drank, we placed each empty can in the dark square in the woodwork. Clutching our final can apiece in our hands, we jumped as the heavy rap sounded on the outer door.

"Open up, you guys!" screamed Mark.

Quickly we set the half-full cans on the inner ledge and put the mirror back in place. We popped a Certs into our mouths.

"Hurry up!" Mark continued. "What's taking you so long?"

Ed opened the door. "Oh, hi, Mark. What's up?"

"You know what's up. You're under arrest. Where's the beer?"

"Beer?" asked Ed calmly. "You must be kidding. It's against dorm rules."

"Yeah, well, you got it in here," he said. "I know, 'cause he doesn't always look like <u>that</u>."

It was true. Paul was sitting slumped in the big lounge chair, one long leg draped casually over the armrest. His normally neat, black hair hung suspiciously over his right eye. His cheerful grin, a common characteristic, looked pasted on. Both eyes were glazed.

"Besides, I can smell it."

"It's my laundry," said Ed. "I haven't done a wash in three weeks. I've been studying too much."

"Don't feed me that crap. Let me smell your breath." Mark grabbed Ed's collar and pulled him close. Ed breathed slowly into his face.

"Candy. Some mint. You guys are all chewing mints. Every single one of you."

"Is there a dorm rule against eating mints?"

"Shut up, wise guy!" Mark snapped. "By the power vested in me by the office of the dean of men, I demand to search this room."

"Be my guest."

After a lengthy search accompanied by assorted curses, Mark turned to four smiling freshmen. "All right," he began.

"You win. So, I'll leave you with this warning. I'm going to keep my eyes and ears open, and if I ever catch you troublemakers doing anything wrong, I'll take you to the highest court on campus. Now, if you've got any beer in here, I suggest you get it out of here fast."

After Mark slammed the door, which was clearly against dorm regulations, we finished our beers, concealed the evidence, and said our goodnights. Paul and I walked to our respective rooms under the watchful eye of Super Proctor, who was hiding in the broom closet.

As Don and Ed settled down to sleep, they were jolted awake by the sound of their door crashing in, revealing Mark's fat stomach shining in the light from the hall. "Aha! I got you!"

Don, who was blind without his glasses, shouted, "Who is it?"

"Who do you think it is?"

Mark had launched one final attack. As he plodded off down the hall, the sound of the boys' howling laughter echoed in his embarrassed ears. He ignored the inclination to issue a noise warning and fine.

****

After the "sergeants" came the "majors" in each dorm. These were the dorm president, vice-president, and secretary-treasurer, who did nothing except run for election once a year. It was no coincidence that half the kids didn't know what positions they occupied. And those were the kids who voted.

The three "majors" were powerless puppets controlled, along with everyone else, by the sole "general." This was the house mother, our leader. Nilo was blessed with the spirit of Ma Tubes, as she came to be known because of her passion for television. Whenever somebody stopped into her apartment on the first floor, she would be found sitting in stony silence absorbing the rays of the boob tube. She would finally acknowledge the person's presence with a subdued "hello," conclude whatever business was necessary, and return to her isolation chamber.

She ruled the dorm with an iron fist, however. She was a Puritan from the word "go." If Jonathan Edwards was still alive, she'd be his biggest fan. She loved to make sneak attack on guys in their rooms – apparently during reruns. She surprised a freshman one day who was sitting in a chair browsing through a huge stack of pornography. She dragged him downstairs, threw the magazines into her fireplace, and telephoned his mother long distance in Colorado.

As much as we were wary of Ma Tubes for her prying nature, she was generally tolerated by the boys in Nilo. Such was not the case in neighboring Maner Hall. I could never figure out how the hall got its name. It looked more like a tenement slum than a "manor", and the guys who lived there had no "manners" at all. One irate mother, upon inspecting her son's newly assigned room in the basement of Maner Hall, charged head first into the office of President Skanks. Having interrupted him while he was smoking a cigar and reading Sports Illustrated, she told him her son would be placed in another dorm immediately. She finished her tirade by saying, "I don't know when you were last out of your castle to inspect the peasant's dwellings, but one of them is a crumbling, filthy old barn sitting in the middle of a drainage ditch."

No one before or since has ever more accurately described Maner Hall, but it suited the guys that lived there. They enjoyed tearing up the furniture in the TV room, ripping the screens out of the windows and hurling them down on unsuspecting passersby, and generally destroying the already desolate atmosphere. Their recently hired house mother, Ma Watson, was an absolute terror. Determined to put a stop to their wild shenanigans, she would run through the dorm, screaming at the boys and fining them. This went on from the time she arrived in September to the fateful night in October when the morons rushed her to an early retirement.

She was just settling down that night, when a loud crash in her living room roused her. She hurried out of her bedroom and switched on the hall light. Her one long, piercing scream carried out into the cold night air. Stuck halfway through her battered front door was a piano with an embryo pig resting on the keys. A knife had been stuck first through a scrawled note and next through the side of the pig. The note read, "You're next, Ma."

Chapter 4 – The First Fall

There were a thousand new things to experience that fall. I had played high school football and baseball – neither very well – so it seemed only natural to try something different. Soccer was a sport that wasn't offered in my high school. In fact, it wasn't offered in any high school. When I jogged out to the grassy field in my brand-new Adidas cleats for my first afternoon practice, I had played soccer only once before in my entire life. I had a lot to learn.

Soccer had been started at the Hilltop one year before I arrived. It was a "club" and was not officially recognized as a sport, except by those who ran around for two hours five nights a week in the sweltering heat or the freezing cold. The athletic director wasn't even going to allow soccer to be used as a suitable substitute for the P.E. requirement. After all, he reasoned, our coach wasn't a coach at all, but rather the school's registrar. The fact that he played on a semi-pro team in Cedar Rapids, well, it didn't matter. He must have been more intelligent, too. He convinced the P.E. coaches that playing soccer was more physically strenuous than jumping jacks and assorted games such as bombardment and medicine ball.

Soccer was definitely a sport. The foreign kids who were raised on soccer used their feet gracefully, as if they were extensions of their hands. The poor American kids, brought up on baseball, had to cover their shortcomings with sheer power. Consequently, American soccer was a combination of football and hockey, but there were no pads. The only thing they had in common was the bumps, bruises, and blood.

In the first fall I played the sport, I received numerous scrapes and cuts. This was part of the game. It went with the wind at your front, the mud in your cleats, and the rain in your face. I was seriously injured twice. One wound came during an actual game.

During a crucial contest with Markland College, I was deftly removed from action by a rival who must have once played Paul Bunyan in his high school theatre. He drove his massive shoulder halfway through my chest, sending me flying to the ground. I was stunned.

As I rolled in agony on the turf, I was aware of a buzzing in my ear. I finally recognized this as the referee's voice saying, "You'll be all right. Don't worry, you'll be fine." That was easy for him to say. It was hard for me to say it. In fact, it was hard for me to say anything.

I tried to yell "internal injury," but nothing came out. I'm glad for that now. It would have been pretty inane to yell something medical at a time like that. I was afraid that if they didn't send for an ambulance immediately, it would be too late.

Suddenly, the pain subsided. A great relief spread over me; I only had the wind knocked out of me. I didn't need a stretcher, much less an ambulance. I walked off the field under my own power. As for the cheering crowd, some idiot yelled, "Watch out for those low bridges."

The ribs were bruised enough to keep me out of action for a week. The aftermath of the injury saw me wearing a chest support to help me breathe without pain. I recovered sufficiently before the next game, however. I didn't dare show up prepared to watch the game from the sidelines out of uniform and wearing my brace. The joker in the crowd would have shouted, "Nice bra. Are you modeling for the catalogue?"

My all-time worst injury occurred in practice. I charged Francis Chong, a foreign-born player with legs like trees, as he was preparing to kick the cover off the ball. The ball exploded upward as if shot from a cannon, travelled a good three yards, and nestled squarely in my groin. Play was instantly stopped by the scream heard 'round the world. It was a time unequaled in the history of pain. I would have fainted, but I was positive that I would never regain consciousness. So, I fought my way back up toward the bright light in the sky, which must have been the sun, although I remember a cloudy day.

As I crawled off the field, those three ageless questions raced through my mind. Am I still alive, will I ever be able to have kids, and what good are those athletic supporters, anyhow? The answers: who cares, I'm not married so it doesn't matter, and just think where I'd be now without one.

****

Four or five doors banged open and six or eight guys pounded down the iron-grey stairwell and exploded out the front door of Nilo Hall. A passing motorist saw ragged sweatshirts and torn jeans race swiftly across the street and heard tennis shoes crunch through fallen leaves en route to a game of touch football on a warm autumn afternoon. Only minutes before, fourth floor Nilo had shook with excitement as one of us rounded up the others. Books and studies were carelessly abandoned. Something told us that this golden afternoon – one that was repeated often – was not to be wasted, because it would never be with us again.

For the next two hours, the happy sweat rolled off our shining faces as football rhetoric filled the air. The feel of leather in our hands merged with the sound of our shoes hitting the hard ground and the distant smell of burning leaves. When the last touchdown was scored, we trudged up the hillside, licking salty drops of sweat off the corners of our mouths and matching big plays with the grass stains on our knees. The autumn wind caught our laughter and kept it forever.

****

Besides football, there were other ways to relax when not studying. Before college, it was unusual for me to take walks, mainly because in Chicago's suburbs the scenery was dull, the sky was gray, and it was against the law to burn leaves. Street walks were avoided at all costs. With traffic always present, a person ran the risk of being run down by a driver who just had to be somewhere for no particular reason.

But my friends and I walked the quiet streets of Pleasant Valley without fear. It was a refreshing sojourn to the little town on a cool October day. The afternoon sun peeked through the bright orange and yellow leaves, leaving jigsaw patches of light against the dark background of the red-brick streets. The locals stopped their day's activities for a brief chat or a friendly smile as we window shopped along Main Street. We watched the old man who ran the Strand Theatre change the billing for the week by taking down the glass window and filling the metal squares with a new set of pictures. Occasionally, the day's highlight came with a pause at the bakery and the purchase of a half-dozen doughnuts fresh from the oven.

At night, the cold, crisp wind whipped the branches back and forth, causing the eerie shadows of late October to dance menacingly through the streets. Everywhere were signs of Halloween. Witches, ghosts, goblins, and skeletons peered out from doors and windows and moaned at those who crossed their pathways. We decided to celebrate by going from house-to-house singing pumpkin carols – we figured we were too old for trick or treat. Plans were finalized as the sinister holiday approached.

The scheme worked out very nicely. Dennis, Mike, Paul, Don, Arnie, and I went out into the night. Taking the president's wife at her word, we paid an impromptu visit to the huge white house on the hill, where we were treated to delicious - although slightly stale - brownies. Singing and eating our way around town, we had a marvelous time for most of the evening.

The night nearly ended on a sour note, however. We approached one green-tinted house with a lighted front porch. Two live goblins, one male and one female, watched us carefully as we walked up the narrow front path. Their eager eyes did not blink and their little bodies did not move from the window.

Suddenly, all hell broke loose. The little girl ran screaming into the bowels of the house. As I began my soliloquy, her voice could be heard coming from far within. "Daddy," she yelled, "there's a bunch of big boys outside!"

Frozen in terror, my comrades watched the front door swing open, revealing barking dogs and a shadowy figure that appeared to be a man with a rifle in his hands. As the two puppies flew past us, the man with the evil face stepped out into the light. He raised the metal broom in his hand. Suddenly, he smiled. "Hey, come here, everybody. It's a bunch of kids singin' carols."

A country family materialized from out of the woodwork. Ma, pa, brother, sister, gram, gramp, aunts, uncles, nephews, and nieces cheered wildly through our set and sang along on the encore. We trekked home to bed, thankful that this wasn't the big city, or the dogs would have been Dobermans and the broom would have been a shotgun.

****

The mid-term was coming. Frank Soader, a country boy who did everything infinitely slower than the rest of the world, lived down the hall in room 412. We walked back and forth to the history course we had both foolishly enrolled in that first semester. Together, we sweated through volumes of reading about Oliver Cromwell. Neither of us had time to finish the last book, which described the social customs and mores of the day, before the mid-term exam. We assumed we could dodge any question which dealt with this material. As we walked through the October rain following the test, we discussed it.

"Cheez, that was a bear."

"Oh," moaned Frank as he plodded along through the puddles, "I don't know if I passed it."

"I think we made it. That was nice of him to give us four out of six."

"Yeah," said Frank. "I took the first three for sure, but I didn't know which one to do after that. So, I wrote on the social customs one."

"You what?"

"I wasn't too sure what to write," he added.

"Well, I'm not surprised. Don't you remember? We didn't even read that book. You can't bullshit your way through a college exam. This isn't high school, you know."

Frank got 20 out of 25 on the last question. I received 10 on the one I chose to answer. As a result, I scored a C+; he got a B-. I was right. This wasn't high school.

Chapter 5 – Sex and the Single Freshman

It didn't make any difference which college I attended. I had looked several campuses over with a careful eye. They all featured the curriculum I was most interested in studying: women. These were not high school girls either; they were college women. They were free, eligible, wild, exciting, sensuous females of the world.

We sat around in Nilo for weeks sizing up the scouting sheet for prospects. Fresh Faces was the sex manual published by the college to help direct the freshmen toward possible mates. The illustrated guide included every freshman's name, hometown, and campus address. It was fun trying to find a match for a beautiful young girl seen earlier that day in a class. Unfortunately, most of the pictures were high school senior shots in dress clothes. The guys had crew cuts, and the girls had permanents. In Fresh Faces, even Eunice looked ravishing.

There were few opportunities to ask girls out, however, unless you used the phone. This technique was dangerous at best, because if a guy's choice wasn't home, her roommate invariably was. Being forced to leave a message gave away the advantage of surprise, which was a considerable one when trying to land that first date. Most girls were smart enough to reason that boys weren't calling them to get an assignment. By the time the second call was placed, she had ample time to fabricate a good excuse. She was sorry, of course, but she had to study for the biology test next month, or she had to go home for her sister's wedding.

A girl could really turn the tables if she never wanted the boy to call again. She would boldly walk up to him when he was surrounded by his friends and say, "Hey, my roommate told me you called this afternoon. I was out. What was it you wanted, anyway?"

"Oh, nothing much," the red-faced boy would reply, as his friends laughed their guts out behind his back. "I just wanted to know what the English assignment was for tomorrow. That's all."

"You should pay attention in class. The last half of Moby Dick. Good luck. I've finished it already."

I was too clever to be outfoxed in that manner. I figured if I gave a girl time to think about going out with me, it would be another boring night in the library. It was hard to catch a girl on campus long enough to ask her out. Only a brave guy could ask a new girl out while standing in the lunch line.

I needed more time for . . . Karen Walter. The girl of my dreams. While awake, I saw her three times a week – MWF from 1:00 to 1:50 in Speech Communication 101. In the small class of thirteen, I watched her every move. I secretly applauded her dark hair, green eyes, and angelic voice. When it was her turn to speak, she floated past my desk, leaving the scent of her perfume clinging to my nostrils.

I wanted to take her out in the worst way, but she always walked to class with her good friend. I did say "hi" to her once. Everyone had to go around the room and say something nice to each other. Working my way toward her, I came face-to-face with Paul Mathews, winked, and said, "I get to talk to Karen. What'll I say?"

"Tell her you think she has a very pleasant speaking voice. She'll like that."

Two more handshakes. One step to go. Bingo. I looked calmly into her eyes and exclaimed, "Hi, Karen. I think you're the most beautiful girl in the world."

"Why, thank you," she giggled. "I thought you were very funny the other day when you sneezed during your speech."

That irritated me. I hadn't even sneezed.

I sat down. I was crestfallen. Karen Walter had sneered at me. Let's face it, I didn't have a chance. She was much too beautiful for my likes ... and too graceful, too charming ...

Professor Chester was speaking. What was he saying?

My golden chance had finally arrived. He had paired Karen up with me for an interview, to be conducted in front of the class. After class, we met and set up a meeting for the next afternoon in the lounge of her dorm. Practice makes perfect. We would be perfect on speech day.

The bright sun radiated down from the brilliant blue Iowa sky as I hurried briskly across campus. This would be a glorious day for me, I thought. The mild weather said so. At some point in the flowing conversation, I would pop the magic question to Karen, and she would say yes. One Friday night would pile onto another, and the long chain of dates would blend into a solid love affair. She would soon want no other man.

Karen escorted me into the lounge and gestured to one of the small couches. "Why don't we sit over here?" she said. "I think we'll be more comfortable."

"But first," I said boldly, "shouldn't you change into something more comfortable?"

"What?" she said crossly.

"Nothing."

"Look, let's get started," she said. "I haven't got all day."

We sat in one of the many plush sofas. The huge fireplace at the far end stared quietly out at the room. Overall, it was a giant step up from the beat-up furniture in the lounges of the boys' dorms. I settled back in my seat, only slightly nervous with apprehension. I had nearly blown it. How could I be so stupid?

We asked the questions with ease, and I was feeling much more relaxed. As we progressed, I knew my time was running out. I had to ask Karen out for Friday night.

"Well, I guess we're done," she said. "Anything else?"

"Well . . ." I hesitated. Sweat poured off my face in little rivers. Karen was looking right at me with those gorgeous green eyes, waiting suspiciously for my next question. Had she guessed what was coming?

"Well . . ."

"That does it," Karen exploded. "I haven't got oodles of time." Staring a hole through me, she said, "If you're trying to ask me out, the answer is yes. If you're trying to conduct a serious interview, you're heading toward a sure D, 'cause your questions are lame."

That was all there was to it. I had my first college date. Karen Walter, one of the most beautiful girls on campus, had asked herself out for me and accepted. And I had been worried. I sure knew how to pick 'em. Some ordinary girl might have cracked under the strain. But not old Karen. She was first-class all the way.

****

The Strand. The most unique movie theatre in the whole world. Built in 1927, the same year "The Jazz Singer" starring

Al Jolson was released, its red-brick front bravely faced the cold Iowa winters and wet Iowa springs year after year. The marquee never listed the current feature. Surrounded by white light bulbs, it always read simply "The Strand." To find out what was showing from week to week, one had to walk up to the giant glass window and look at studio shots that advertised the various movies. The film was "Wait Until Dark," a spooky thriller starring Audrey Hepburn.

I proudly approached the ticket taker's window at 6:45 on Friday night with Karen Walter by my side. The old lady's weathered smile greeted me. I slipped her two dollars – a buck for each of us. Her husband held the door open and took our tickets. We were ushered into the lobby, where we were treated to the aroma of fresh popcorn. Deciding against a snack for the moment, we made our way through the red velvet curtains into the old movie house.

One word adequately described the interior: narrow. I had been in wider closets. The large center section consisted of six seats across, with two "lovers'" seats on either side. We chose the two-seaters halfway down on the left. It made me feel more secure. To get past me now, Karen had to either go over me or through the wall. Those were my kind of odds.

Karen turned to me, her soft hair brushing against my arm. I smiled at her.

"Nice place, isn't it?"

"Yes," I said. "It's not very wide, though."

"This theatre reminds me of a bus."

"A bus? Oh, no, not a bus. I can see quite a few different things here, but definitely not a bus."

Actually, it was the most intelligent idea either of us had expressed all evening. I was just arguing with her for the sake of arguing.

As I was sitting reflecting on how much the theatre looked like a bus, the lights dimmed and the show began. Prior to the feature film, the Strand always showed a short, a cartoon, and coming attractions, just like the good old days.

"Would you care for something to eat or drink before the feature starts?" I asked politely.

"No, thank you," Karen responded.

We sat in silence as the picture began. "Wait Until Dark" was a good movie, with Audrey Hepburn playing a blind woman who carried, unbeknownst to her, a doll with smuggled heroin stashed in it. Alan Arkin headed a team of criminals who stalked the poor blind woman for the doll. Just as the climax was coming, I got a coughing spell. Oh, brother, what should I do now?

"I'm going out for a pop," I coughed relentlessly. "You want anything?"

"No," she said, her mind on the picture.

I shot rapidly up the aisle and into the tiny lobby. I reached into my pocket and withdrew the small, shiny coin. I smiled. Where else could one find a pop machine where drinks were only a dime? I turned the black plastic knob to GRAPE and slipped the dime into the slot.

I watched the cup fill with purple liquid. I grabbed it, took a quick sip, and my cough began to ease. I thought about Karen. I hoped she was having a good time. Oh, well, it was time to liven it up. I would walk back to our seats, sit down beside her, and casually drape my arm over her.

I walked. I sat. I started to drape my arm over her.

I don't know if you're aware of the only scene which is bound to scare the life out of you. It's after the blind woman has knifed the head psychopath, tries to get out the door and cannot, and makes her way to the bottom of the steps. Then he lunges at her, grabbing her ankle, and causing the entire audience to jump and scream.

Karen did likewise, causing my grape pop to spill and stain my white Levis.

As we made our way out of the theatre, the crowd's muffled laughter rang in my ears. I wished the bus would stop so I could get off.

Chapter 6 – Bored Job

A middle-income family in 1968 has seldom been able to afford the entire tuition, fees, and room and board of a private college. Thirty-two hundred dollars must be set aside annually, or other arrangements must be made. My family needed to make other arrangements. I was forced to rely on part scholarship, part parental assistance, part work like a fiend all summer long, and part work loan on campus.

The latter was a system which enabled students to earn money for a required number of hours per week. The money was in the form of a board job contract, the total sum of which was never seen by the student. I worked six days a week at a whopping one dollar and thirty cents an hour.

I was immediately integrated into the largest enterprise on campus, FSOA, the food factory, which served twenty-one meals a week. The initials stood for Food Service of America. The food, believe it or not, was better than that served by many other colleges. FSOA had its little surprises, such as meatloaf without the meat, beef stroganoff without the beef, and only four types of drinks: milk, diet milk, chocolate milk, and water. (Today's campuses have tea, ice tea, lemonade, and any type of pop, plus the milk.) Most of the food was good, however, and we could eat as much as we wanted every meal.

Pound for pound and gas pain for gas pain, breakfast was the best meal of the day. The big five headed up the morning menu: scrambled eggs, French toast, pancakes, bacon, and sausages.

Breakfast was not only the tastiest meal, it was also the easiest one to work. Less than half the campus attended, even though it had been paid for in the lump sum for room and board. So, there was less work to do than at the crowded luncheon meal or the waited dinner meal in the evening. Consequently, I signed up for the breakfast shift.

"Big" Bob Beeley was the boss man. He ran the show at FSOA. His jovial personality and exuberant laugh were counterbalanced by his foreman Dick Sharp. Dick was a short man with sunken eyes, a five o'clock shadow, and a nervous laugh which was always chopped off as soon as it began. It was just as well. He really wasn't funny. He tried to impress me with his overall knowledge and efficiency on my first day of work when he introduced me to the breakdown line. (Breakdown = break down the dishes, silverware, etc.)

"Okay, Tiger, you'll be working here on the breakdown line every morning. We'll give you Sunday off." He started to laugh, but stopped abruptly. "You see this switch here? This turns the belt on."

I watched as the long conveyor belt moved noisily past the narrow water trough.

"Now, there'll be four of you on this team. You'll all stand along here. As each tray goes by, you will be responsible for different items. For example, let's say you're up here at the front. A tray goes by. You grab the silverware, the coffee cup, and the napkin. Put the silverware in this tub, the coffee cup in this rack, and throw the napkin under here in this garbage can. We don't save the paper napkins once they've been used." Once again, he started to laugh, then stopped. "Any questions so far, Tiger?"

"Yeah, why do you call me Tiger? I have a name. It's Sean."

"Oh, that. I call all my workers Tiger. You'll get used to it."

(Why? I don't know.)

Moving quickly down the line, he pointed out the other positions to me. "If you work here, you grab the glasses, here the little saucers and bowls, and down here the big plates and trays. Now, you're probably thinking that's the easiest. But, oh, no. This is the key to the whole operation. This is the quarterback. Only a senior can handle this position. You're only a freshman, aren't you? I won't have a speck of trouble out of you, will I?"

"No."

"Good. Now, where was I? Oh, yes, this job. Mark Thomas. A senior. Bet you were wondering why everything's set up so neat. Mark done that. Every morning at six-thirty sharp, he sets 'er up. Then he goes to eat. He'll be back in a minute. He's your crew leader. He takes the responsibility for setting things up. Then, when this whole line is full of trays, he works down at the end here. See, if the tray pushes against these two bars here, bingo, the line stops. The job is to keep the line moving. Only one man can do that. This man at the end. He's the quarterback. Also, when these buckets of glasses, silverware, bowls, saucers, and plates are full, he shoves 'em on an empty tray and sticks 'em into this elevator. They go down to the basement. Know what's down there?"

I took a wild guess. "The dishwashing room?"

Dick laughed, and stopped. "We just call it the dish room," he said. "But you'll catch on to it. Know what we call the breakdown line here?"

"No," I answered politely.

He smiled for a minute and then said, "The breakdown line."

Boy, this guy was a barrel of laughs.

"One more thing. This trough here is for food. Not everybody cleans their plates. If you're working plates - which you won't 'cause you're not a senior - just scrape the extra food right into the water here. Now, this is the garbage disposal. Don't take time to push the food in there as you go along. If things are crowded, just keep the line moving. Remember, this is a major operation. It'll pile up a bit, but don't mind the smell. You'll get used to it. When you get a break, just take your hand and shove it right down the trough into the disposal. Don't be bashful. Just use your hands. You can wash them afterwards. And make sure no silverware gets caught in there. If it busts up, we have to get a man to fix it."

Things went well. I stood in front of the line and gathered in silverware, coffee cups, and napkins, and I didn't save the napkins. I enjoyed the job, and contrary to public opinion, it wasn't a major operation. After the rush before eight o'clock classes on MWF, there was little to do. We'd play broom hockey with an orange if things were dull.

Halfway through the semester, we lost our senior breakdown leader, whom nobody talked to anyway. Quiet Mark Thomas didn't show up one October morning, because he joined about twenty-five other students in an Administration building takeover. At the time, this was a fairly new form of campus entertainment, although it would soon become more popular. The purpose of the nonviolent seizure of the building was to force social, cultural, and curriculum changes that would benefit the black students on campus. Mark and other whites helped out, mostly because there were only twenty blacks on campus, and they couldn't launch a massive riot with such small numbers. So, the landmark black takeover actually involved more white students. Nothing major developed; everyone was led peacefully into a waiting police wagon, and some curriculum changes were made for the following semester. The social and cultural changes were unfortunately still light-years away. Although more than half the blacks on campus did not participate in the demonstration, they were permanently linked with the incident. Within two years, the black population on campus would dwindle to under ten.

The immediate problem of that morning greeted me when I arrived at my job. The breakdown line was not set up. As I tried to set up for the very first time, Dick Sharp told people to pile the trays up and make more work for the irresponsible young boys who didn't show up on time. Berserk with anger, Dick was ranting at me while neglecting to admit that Mark was at fault for not showing up at all. I calmly took my time gathering the necessary items in the basement of the Union.

When I got upstairs, there was Dick, whose brain had snapped, trying to clear off about fifty trays that were piled in a disheveled fashion across the frozen breakdown line. He was flinging food against the wall, breaking dishes in the trough, and shouting obscenities at the top of his lungs.

I don't think poor Dick ever recovered. He must have been mentally unstable to begin with, for he had a meeting with "Big" Bob Beeley, who wasn't pleased. Dick was dismissed from his duties and never seen on the Hilltop again. Way to go, Tiger!

I convinced "Big" Bob to let the three of us continue on the line without naming a replacement for Mark. Kevin, Neil, and I felt we could handle the job without a new fourth man. "Big"

Bob agreed. From that point on, it was super. We shifted back and forth to help each other, and if the line stopped during the rush, we would all count "one-two-three" until it started moving again. It seldom stopped.

Neil did have one little problem adjusting to the "quarterback" position. He was responsible for sending buckets full of glasses, silverware, bowls, saucers, and plates down to the dish room. When the tray reached the basement, it was removed by the dish crew. The elevator continued downward, where the two metal sides broke apart and journeyed up their respective sides independent of each other.

Everything worked fine unless one of the metal halves, a crude holder, was broken. This left an empty space and made it quite impossible for a tray to balance on one edge. Neil had a tendency to shove a tray in without looking, a bad mistake for a rookie who wanted to keep the line moving at any cost. The cargo would plunge, sailing past the dish room and crashing loudly and horribly to its death in the "pit."

Although a costly error, this might not have been such a dangerous one had it not been for the odd desire of dish room workers to flirt with fate. This was done by taking turns sticking their heads into the elevator shaft and looking up to see if any trays were coming down. If one was rocketing down the chute, the gory effect would be not unlike a guillotine. It would take a brave person with a strong stomach to clean out the "pit" that evening.

****

The breakfast crew, person for person, was the funniest of any shift. This was probably due to the fact that, when the rush was over, we all had to find ways to amuse ourselves.

Also, we had to get out of bed every morning between six-thirty and seven. This tends to make one a bit lightheaded.

Zany Zelda was the star of the show. She worked out front on the serving line. Her shocking red hair and crazy laugh was how she got her nickname, and she had no trouble keeping us in stitches.

She loved to come back to visit us at work and tell us how we were so funny. Whenever we left the breakdown line unattended during slow times to wander out and have a little food, she would sneak back and take coffee cups and glasses out of the racks and put them back on the belt. Then, she would run out, screaming in her high-pitched voice, "Boys, boys, hurry up! Quick! It's a rush! It's a rush!"

We would hurry back to see a bunch of cups and glasses travelling slowly by our posts. She'd laugh like a hyena and tell us how funny we all looked racing back there. It was times like these when we thought Zelda would make a good dish room helper – especially at the elevator.

She laughed at her own mistakes, too. She dropped an entire tray of juice glasses once, and as she jumped out of the way, her left foot was soaked by the grape-colored liquid. She walked around laughing all day, pointing out the inconsistency in her otherwise sterile white outfit. "Look at this, will ya? Can you dig that crazy purple shoe?"

I laughed and said, "You look real nice that way, Zelda."

"That's nothing. I've got another pair like these at home."

The only time we ever saw her angry was when Kevin made an error in judgment. The elevator was used to send food and beverages up from the basement. Zelda would send empty carts down and expect them to come up full. If things weren't moving, it didn't take her long to get on the phone to the kitchen crew. "What's the matter with you cooks down there? We're out of pancakes and sausages. Send some up right away. And make hurry about it!"

Once, after one of her insane babblings, the elevator opened, exposing the same two empty carts that Zelda had sent down earlier. She was livid with rage, and decided to go down for a direct confrontation.

There were two things wrong with the elevator. One was its average speed, which was so slow one never knew if the elevator was moving. It was faster to go outside the Union and scale the brick wall. The other fault was the lack of space within. If there were two food carts inside, there was only room for two people, and only if they stood with their backs plastered against the carts and their noses pressed snugly to the closed doors.

Zany Zelda, with fire in her eyes, jumped into the elevator, pressed her back against the carts, and pushed the red button for down. Kevin, with a single bowl of fruit in his hand, rounded the corner and headed straight for the elevator, determined to get in before the doors closed. As the doors began to slide together, only Kevin's hand with the bowl of fruit was inside. He withdrew his hand quickly, leaving the fruit bowl inside; it landed down the front of Zelda's dress. As Kevin fled in terror to hide under the breakdown line, we could hear Zelda's muffled screams coming from below.

"Aaaaaaaah! I'm gonna kill you – whoever you are!"

Unlike her attention for her stained shoe, Zany Zelda's reaction to her wet front was a silent one. As Kevin carefully concealed himself in back the remainder of the morning, she patrolled the serving area with quiet dignity, seemingly unaware of the stifled laughter behind her back.

Neil, who did not share Kevin's fear, put a red towel on his head, shoved two grapefruits under his white kitchen coat, and covered the chest area with water. "Hey, boys! Dig these fruity boobs, will ya?"

Chapter 7 – The Ice Age

I was going to go home on Thanksgiving break. This was a four-day vacation never officially recognized by the college, as Friday and Saturday classes were still in session. Most of the kids took off anyway.

Dennis and I waited for my father to pick us up, and we were out of there. After dropping Dennis off, and a quick trip to the barber shop – "You wouldn't want your mom to see you in that condition" – we arrived home. I'll never forget my first trip into my bedroom. It was so small. And this was before my brother had rearranged the room to suit his taste.

The Beatles had released an album, called simply "The White Album" by its fans. It was a double album, and all 30 songs were brand-new. And contrary to the colorful pictures on the last two albums, it was all white, front and back, with only the title – "The Beatles" – raised in white. My sister, my brother, and I rested on the floor with the lyric sheet spread out in front of us and cranked those tunes. It was the first album of the year by the group, and The Beatles were definitely back.

****

A winter chill signaled the arrival of our journey back to the Hilltop. A giant Christmas tree was raised from the orange carpet to the ceiling of the Union, spreading its massive branches over two and a half floors of the building. This barren evergreen welcomed the students back from Thanksgiving. The decorating of the tree was left entirely to the student body, a tradition which was celebrated as an all-night ritual complete with hot chocolate, cookies, and Christmas carols.

Ornaments and lights were hung over the great body of the tree, and a final star was placed on top by a brave student balanced high atop an aluminum ladder. Dummy presents in bright wrappings were arranged beneath the sagging lower limbs. The total effect was one of breathtaking splendor. Extra fir branches were draped over ledges and doorways until the Union smelled of a sweet pine aroma.

The final touch of Christmas on campus greeted my astounded eyes early in December as I walked out into the cold evening air from an afternoon of study in the library. Looking straight up, I saw the brightly colored Christmas lights surrounding the steeple of the Chapel. As the students made their way toward the Union for dinner at six, the sounds of Christmas carols could be heard as the old Chapel bells rang out the melodies.

****

With mountains of soft snow covering the ground, we turned indoors for recreational activity. Dennis, Mike, Paul, Don, Arnie, and I were the basketball freaks of fourth floor, and we assumed that the boys' gym, which was situated across the street from Nilo, would be the ideal place to play. There was a problem, however. It was used all day for gym classes and, in the late afternoon, for practice sessions by the basketball team, after which it was locked up securely for the night. That left Saturday; several of us cut classes.

The six of us entered the gym at eight o'clock one Saturday morning only to be confronted by the head custodian, Mr. Black. "And where do you think you're going?"

I thought he wasn't the brightest man in the world, and now I was fairly sure of it. Where else would six boys dressed in shorts and gym shoes, carrying a basketball be going? And we <u>were</u> in the lobby of a gymnasium.

"We're going to play basketball," said Paul.

The immense forehead beneath the short grey hair bulged out as he puffed on a reeky cigar. He eyed us carefully, squinting at each of us in turn. "The hell you are."

"Why can't we play?" I asked.

"Because I'm just here to clean up the place for the swim meet this afternoon. I'm leaving at ten and locking up behind me."

"Great," I said sarcastically. "How come nothing's ever open around here? What about tomorrow?"

"This place is closed all day Sundays," he said. "We can't just leave it wide open, you know. Something might get stolen."

Yeah, I thought, like one of the backboards.

"We should be able to play here whenever we want," I said bravely. "We pay a lot of money to go to this school, and the facilities should be available."

"Is that so? Listen, young man, I'm in charge here. Now don't you get smart with me."

I was happy Paul stepped in. He was the tallest member of our group and presented a figure of leadership which might be enough to bluff old Mr. Black. Besides, he had a knack for sliding over crucial situations with a politician's smile, never antagonizing his opponent.

"Now, Mr. Black," he began, "let's be sensible. You have to leave at ten, but there's no good reason why we can't play upstairs while you're cleaning up the pool area. We won't cause you a bit of trouble, and we'll leave right at ten."

"Well, I don't know." His brow showed lines of deep concentration. "I'm supposed to sweep the gym floor, too. Now, if you'd be willing to do that for me, I might just decide to overlook the fact that you're not supposed to be in here."

"What do you mean? We have a right to be in here!" I yelled.

"Quiet!" Paul grabbed my arm to silence me. "Do you want to play or not? We'll sweep the floor. Where are the brooms?"

"Now, that's more like it," he said. We followed him to a nearby closet. He produced two big brooms, which he handed to us. "Take turns. And remember, I'm doing you a big favor."

So that was that. We reluctantly swept the floor so we could be allowed to play basketball in facilities that should have been open to the general student body, not just the athletes. I never understood the policy of the athletic director, who was also head basketball coach. But the man was never more correct than when I overheard him tell a prominent alumnus, "Only the best athletes play on that court."

****

Winter on campus held many new surprises for the freshmen. There were additional campus and dorm rules to be learned and obeyed. Snowballing was illegal to the tune of twenty-five dollars, and fifty dollars was the price for an errant snowball which made contact with a lamp or window. There was, however, a monstrous snowball-fight every winter: the annual Nilo-Maner battle.

The battleground was the open field across the street next to the boys' gym. Only the truly insane participated, and I, being a coward at heart, stayed indoors. I was not alone. Most of the freshmen, frozen in terror, watched from the windows of their rooms as the upperclassmen advanced upon each other with bloodthirsty screams. The speed and accuracy of their missiles was uncanny. The walking wounded, blood spurting from their mouths or noses, made strategic withdrawals to their dorms. The dead lay in lumps on the pink snow, moving occasionally as their frozen bodies were kicked by passing enemies. Those who survived spent the night in celebration, drinking beer until they got sick, recounting old war stories. And people say college kids don't know how to have fun.

The most interesting winter rule was imposed on students by their dorms. During the week of finals, each and every hall became a morgue entitled "Dead House." This simply meant that, since all students were busily cramming for final exams, the dorms must be dead silent at all times. Anyone breathing too loudly on the way to the shower was likely to receive a heavy fine. Mark was having a field day. They were automatic twenty-five dollar fines coupled with ten hours of hard labor in the dorm, such as washing windows or painting walls. These were lonely jobs, too. Not even Tom Sawyer could have persuaded a Nilo man to help out on one of these work details.

The dorms were bitter cold during the winter as well. It wasn't that heat was nonexistent, it was just that it never quite reached the frigid fourth floor. On several occasions, Paul and Mike, who lived on the cold northwest side of the building, had to tack up huge Army blankets over their windows to keep the rush of air out. They went to bed in their jeans and sweatshirts, and tried to sleep through the constant banging of the wind against the windows. The wall thermometer registered a frosty 54 degrees. It was a constant man vs. nature struggle, and nature always won.

On the last Saturday of the semester, the Nilo residents gleefully celebrated together in the annual dormitory Christmas party. The highlight of the evening was the main course, which was lovingly prepared by Ma Tubes. She slaved the entire afternoon over a gigantic pot of her homemade chili. Special herbs and spices were mixed with precision as she concocted the meal. That night, we all swarmed down to the lounge carrying bowls and drinking mugs, which were filled to the brim with piping hot chili. That was the first part of Ma's Christmas gift to the guys. The second part came the following day when two hundred boys had the runs for five hours.

****

The first Christmas vacation was more fun than being at school. As freshmen, we hadn't reached the place where "going home" meant heading back to campus. But after an entire month at home, we were eager to get back. So, a few days after watching the New York Jets destroy the Baltimore Colts in the Super Bowl, we packed up our garments and were ready to return.

Unfortunately, the Wednesday we were scheduled to go back, an ice storm tore viciously across the Midwest. It was not the last frigid blast to hit the Hilltop, either. In four years, I survived at least nine or ten ice storms. They came along with pounds of snow every winter. The normal hills and slopes were turned into roller coaster rides aimed at brick walls or tree trunks. The biting wind came swooping down from Canada, built up speed through Minnesota, and descended upon our faces like knives. During the dreary bleakness of January and February, it was not uncommon to walk backwards from the library to Nilo Hall so as to save one's skin from permanent scars. The calm aftermath of every ice storm presented one of nature's most beautiful pictures, however. The morning sun would sparkle off the silver branches as they chimed rhythmically in the winter breeze.

That day's upheaval was long remembered as one of the most arduous, however. The normal four-hour trip from Chicago's suburbs took six grueling hours. As my father gracefully guided the family Buick through Illinois and Iowa, my mother, Dennis, and I sat on the edges of our seats. We watched huge semis and little foreign cars buckle and spin to their journey's end.

After skillfully succeeding in mastering the slick surface, my father coasted to a stop in front of a nearly abandoned Nilo Hall. We were among the first to arrive. Others would struggle in during late afternoon hours, at various stages of the night, and all through the next day. Paul, who had to finally fly in from St. Louis, arrived late that night in a taxi from Cedar Rapids with a fare of sixteen dollars. Those who came after registration on Thursday were forced to pay the late registration fee of ten dollars, which was not a terrific way to start any semester.

As we carried our baggage up to our room, Dennis almost became the first casualty of the year when he slipped and fell on the ice. It was one of those no-doubt-about-it slammers where the feet skyrocket into the air and the back of the head comes flying down to meet the thick sheet of ice. It was a sickening thud. I have always believed that he wasn't the same after the accident; the collision knocked any functioning brain parts loose for good.

Dennis stopped going to class. He just sat around our room drinking Cokes, reading comics, and complaining of headaches. Because of his fondness for "butting" class and sitting around on his posterior, he became known as Butt-

Butt. This nickname changed gradually. When he chauffeured us around in his old yellow Mustang, he was Bus-Bus; when he got his hair cut, he was Butch-Butch; when he stayed out in the sun too long, he was Burn-Burn; when he threw up his first six-pack of beer, he was Barf-Barf. We would probably have called him Bam-Bam for a few days following his injury on the ice, but no one had thought up the revolving character yet.

After my parents and I helped Dennis up, we continued into the dorm. The inside was unbelievable. Fourth floor shined with its new wax job, and none of us remembered it to be this clean before. The silent tomb exploded as Mike jumped out of 407 and screamed at us suddenly. "Hey, how are you guys?"

We shook hands, gave five, hugged, and jumped around together for several minutes. Mike was human hungry. He had sneaked into the dorm on Sunday, three days ahead of regulation time, and had been hibernating in his room ever since. He would have been happy to see Attila the Hun.

After my parents said good-bye and left to tackle the blizzard once more, Mike, Dennis, and I sat around, told stories, and waited for other people to show up. It wasn't long before we heard an echo of footsteps passing by the door. We could only guess who else had made it through enemy lines into our Alamo. We flung open the door. It was Frank Soader, my old friend from history, standing in front of the door to his room with his father.

"Frank, how're you doing?" I yelled.

"Hey, just great," he said, and greetings were exchanged. "I'd like you all to meet my father, Reverend Soader."

Frank had told us earlier that his father was a Methodist minister, but we had forgotten. Being introduced to a clergyman always made one straighten up quickly. Although Frank's father did not look like the fire and brimstone type, we knew Methodists were down on smoking, drinking, carousing, and generally having fun. So, we secretly figured it would be best to look sharp and act polite.

"Pleased to meet you, sir," I said. "Boy, it sure is good to be back on campus where we can get some serious work accomplished. Right, guys?"

"Oh, yeah," piped up Mike. "I really can't wait until we register. Then, we can buy our books and start studying. I'm getting bored just sitting around thinking about all the work we're going to do. I want to get after it."

An amused smile passed across Reverend Soader's face.

As we stood and waited, Frank turned the key to open room 412. As the door swung open, all eyes were suddenly glued to the ruins within. Frank's roommate Rich, who was the wildest human being this side of Geronimo, had thrown an incredible bash before leaving for Christmas vacation. Bed sheets and pillows were strewn recklessly about the room. Empty beer and booze bottles were resting on every open space of desk and cabinet. Open bags of pretzels and potato chips sat carelessly on chairs and cushions. The final insult, a bra, hung loosely from the post at the head of Rich's bed.

Frozen in stupefied horror, we waited for the wrath of God to come spewing from the stern mouth of Reverend Soader. We cringed noticeably as he began to speak.

"Well," he said quietly, the amused grin back on his face, "it seems to me that you left too early, Frank. It looks like you missed all the fun."

And people say ministers don't have a sense of humor.

Chapter 8 – Rocks in My Head

One of the requirements for graduation, which almost everyone took their first year, was a year of natural science. As far as I was concerned, all the sciences were very unnatural. After no small amount of deliberation and some panic, I decided to enroll in Geology 105. My reasoning behind this choice was simple. I had never taken a course in this subject and knew absolutely nothing about it. I had, on the other hand, taken year-long high school courses in biology, chemistry, and physics, and knew absolutely nothing about them. One way or another, I felt I was ahead of the game by starting fresh with a brand-new science. I would have been better off sticking with the same old embryo pigs or molecular structures.

Professor Bromber and I never got along from the beginning. It took weeks for the easiest lesson to take root in the small space reserved for such subjects. He was convinced that I was not spending enough time studying. Thus, I didn't do very well on his tests.

In all fairness to both parties, I could have spent more time reading, and he could have spent less time lecturing. His lecture notes ran from the time we were seated until five minutes <u>after</u> dismissal time. In eight months, he covered more virgin territory than Lewis and Clark. I think he expected his students to know every rock formation since the beginning of time by the end of the year, and he did his best at cramming the information into our heads. His tests were designed to separate the limestone from the shale, and they usually did the job faultlessly.

By this time, signs of spring were evident all over campus, and I had all the geology I could handle and then some. Springtime on the Hilltop was celebrated in a final flurry of Frisbee and baseball games, trips to the nearby forest preserve for swimming and canoeing, and all-school picnics with foot-long hot dogs and watermelon. All this frivolity was mixed with a sense of sadness that we would soon part with newfound friends and a sense of strain caused by studying for final exams.

Nature lovers were not cheated, either. The geology department saw to that. The annual all-freshmen field trip was planned for the last weekend in April, only two weeks before the semester's end. All three classes, about one hundred and fifty students, were required to attend and take notes. I told Professor Bromber that I would like to be excused to attend a soccer clinic in Cedar Rapids that same Saturday. He politely informed me that I was doing poorly enough as it was and that any hope, however dim, I might have about passing his course would be squelched if I did not go on the trip. He smiled sardonically. I went on the trip.

Don, Dennis, and I were jarred awake by our alarm clocks shortly before five. After showering, we all trudged methodically toward the Union, where the buses were slated to pick us up at five-thirty. None of us were enthused about the proposed starting time. We all thought a few more hours sleep would have been nice, and we were positive of it when we walked out into the chilly morning air and saw the threatening rain clouds above.

"I've got a headache," I mumbled.

"You have those quite often," said Don.

"Yeah. Well, when you throw in rain mixed with geological formations, it's bound to mess your head up," I said.

71

Small groups of zombies staggered from different ends of campus to join the multitude seated on the grassy knoll in front of the Union. Everyone nodded glumly at one another as a sign of recognition.

Shortly before take-off, the big three came toward us from the direction of the Science building. Accompanying Bromber was Hartman, another geology prof, and they were involved in deep conversation. The big smiles on their faces told the story. This excursion meant as much to them as a first trip to a major league baseball game meant to a normal eight-year-old boy. They were wide-eyed as they shared little boy secrets of hidden treasure buried in the rock formations of past civilizations.

Leading them into the land of scientific discovery was the lab assistant known to the freshmen as Quasimodo's sister. Her large frame was covered with a flannel shirt, faded blue jeans, and large climbing boots laced up to her knees. On her back was a giant pack, including a pick and an axe, weighing her down even more. She never walked; she plodded.

She was an impressive leader. It was always a comfort to know that whenever we became too exhausted to crawl another inch, we could look ahead and be inspired to greatness by her forward motion, crushing anything that got in her way. She had trudged silently into previous battles, and we were convinced she would leave no quarry or swamp unconquered.

As the threesome approached the mass of students huddled in small packs, Quasimodo's sister rigidly took her place on the sidewalk. Bromber and Hartman circulated among us, handing out dittoed volumes of information. While casually browsing over the booklet, I was shocked by the word that was typed in capitals and appeared three times on the first page: RATTLESNAKES. Heaven help me. There it was; no doubt about it. We were going into rattlesnake country to look at some stupid rocks. No wonder Quasimodo's sister had on heavy boots. She smiled at me.

"Hey, you guys," I yelled. "Did you see this? Rattlesnakes. We're going to be cut to ribbons. I'm going to die trying to pass this course."

"Oh, c'mon," said Don. "Read more carefully. It says don't get off the trails and into the woods, because there are rattlesnakes in the <u>area</u>."

"Well, we're in the area, too. And a rattlesnake doesn't know the difference between the woods and a path. Their eyesight is only good for an inch off the ground. It's all dirt, leaves, and ankles to them."

"Don't worry," said Dennis. "A snake will get one whiff of your feet and head the other way."

I rolled my eyes. "Oh, you guys are real comedians. Don't tell me we're safe. These geology profs are crazy. They'll go anywhere to get a look at a new bunch of old rocks. What's it to them if they lose a few freshmen on the way? We can't even sue. You know the old saying, dead men tell no tales. In fact, I bet I'll be part of the tour next year. I can see Bromber now, passing out my picture just before the walk among the rattlesnakes starts. 'Extra credit for anyone who can find the fossil of this dead boy. It's only a year old, so it should be clearly visible imbedded in a recent rock bed. It's a sad story. He was our first casualty in over twenty-five years. He went screaming into the woods with a rattlesnake attached to his Achilles tendon. It was right around here somewhere. Poor guy. He wasn't one of our brightest students. He probably didn't read my warning. For those of you who haven't taken the time, it's on page one of your manual.'"

Bob and Bing went into hysterics at the mere mention of my untimely death, so I proceeded to ignore them and got in line for the buses, which were on their way up the Hilltop. The lead bus rounded the curve and churned slowly toward the long line of disillusioned students. Even Don and Dennis were reading their manuals with a more cautious eye than before.

The bus ground to a halt several yards short of the students and cranked its doors open directly in front of Quasimodo's sister. Maybe the bus driver thought she'd eat the bus if he drove past her. Angrily, the students were forced to walk to the waiting vehicle. As soon as we had all climbed aboard one of the three yellow buses, they pulled out into the dark Iowa morning, the rain clouds making it look like night was falling.

As we huddled against the cold wind that whisked at us from seemingly all directions, sleep began to invade our thoughts. My headache was worse due to the bouncing of the bus. So, I slept, my snoring keeping all those around me awake. Suddenly, I was forced to life by the bus jerking to a halt on the gravel that lined the concrete highway. I knew we were nowhere important. It was a field with tall grass and black dirt, and there wasn't a house in sight. I should have guessed that this was the perfect place for lecture number one.

The freezing rain lashed against our frozen faces as Bromber and Hartman took turns rambling on about the significance of the land on which we stood. They informed us that there were definite signs of a great past period, the ice age of North America. It felt like a second ice age was coming.

The rain continued as we stopped a second time, hoping that maybe this time the buses had broken down for good.

Instead, we heard lecture number two about fossils. Here, by the shore of a bubbling river, buried in the rocky ruins were engravings of once living creatures, whose tiny bodies had been permanently etched in stone.

"Spread out, everyone," yelled Professor Hartman. "Start turning those rocks over. There's plenty of fossils to be found."

Apparently, I was one of the chosen people. The first stone I picked up had distinct markings on its back. Wonder of wonders. I had unearthed a recent fossil. Now, this recent fossil, although it sounded impressive, was nothing more than a snail who had expired within the past year. So, I told all my friends about it. The usual response was, "Oh, a dead snail, huh?"

As I was showing it off, my old nemesis, Eunice, happened to spot it. She seemed very interested in it, and since I was going to throw it away, I gave it to her as a keepsake.

I was standing alone staring into the water and rubbing my neck so my headache would leave me. Suddenly, the stillness was shattered by the voice of Bromber in my ear. "You don't look very busy," he said in an annoyed tone. "There are plenty of fossils here if you have the energy to look for them. Or is it merely the desire you lack?"

"I found a recent fossil," I said. "I think it's a dead snail."

All malice was withdrawn from the accusing face of Professor Bromber as he eagerly encouraged me to share my discovery with him. "Where is it? Let me see it."

A black cloud passed across my soul, and I said almost inaudibly, "I gave it to a girl."

It didn't really matter what I did for the rest of the day, or year. I could have discovered dinosaur bones, and Bromber would not have been impressed. In his eyes, I was no more than a heathen who sold his religious medal for a loaf of bread. I was a fallen angel in the kingdom of Bromber. Obviously, the king didn't know Eunice very well.

Lecture number three was given on the side of a twisting highway in the hills of the Mississippi Valley. It was conducted by Professor Hartman. We stood in the wet grass and the humid air as the sun drained the perspiration from our bodies. The mixture of intense heat from the newly arrived sun, and the droning sound of Hartman's voice combined to make me tired and dizzy. I let my body hang limply, and my mind drifted somewhere into outer space. Still standing, I was getting sleepy, sleepy, sleeeeeeeeeepy...

Suddenly, my entire body froze. Sweat poured out of every pore. Twisting my neck, I slowly forced my eyes to travel the entire length of my body, stopping and staring at the object crossing my feet. That one word on page one of the manual flashed before me: RATTLESNAKES.

Gasping, I turned to face Don and Dennis and yelled, "Rattlesnake!"

The entire mass of students reacted as one body – they ran as fast as they could.

Embarrassment overcame fear as the harmless garter snake slithered quickly away into the grass. Bromber rolled his eyes and yelled, "It's only a garter snake. You can stop running." He cast an evil eye my way.

The final stop on the journey was high atop the banks of the Mississippi River. The water itself was miles below us, and the view from the cliff top was majestic. On both sides of the picnic grounds where Hartman spoke was the dense forest where the real rattlesnakes lived.

After his brief talk, the weary travelers gathered hungrily around the truck with the special-delivery lunch courtesy of FSOA. The result of their efforts to provide a tasty picnic lunch was disgusting. The heat had melted the ham and cheese into the dry bun, and it took a stouthearted person to choke down the remains. The warm lemonade was needed to wash down the sandwich. The cookie was simply mush.

The rest of the afternoon was ours to be enjoyed. At least, that was my understanding. But, as we began our hike through the woods, I asked Professor Bromber if we were just supposed to relax and enjoy the scenery from now on and not worry about taking notes.

"Enjoy the scenery and look for rocks," he responded, somewhat disappointed that I still couldn't figure out these simple things for myself.

Knowing full well that the only rock I'd pick up would have a rattlesnake underneath it, I went along with everyone on the hike. It was an uneventful walk, and no harm came to anyone. In fact, it wasn't until we had returned to the buses that Professor Hartman cautioned us not to drink the nearby spring water because it had minerals in it, and we would be sorry twelve hours later. Thanks for the warning.

As the sweltering sun pounded through the bus windows, we bounced home in silence. The headache hammered through my bones. At least I hadn't thrown up yet.

The bus finally stopped. The tired troupe got off.

Professor Bromber let us go with some final words. "Don't forget. Your ten-page paper on this topic is due a week from Monday."

That was it. I found a bush to blow my cookies into.

Chapter 9 – Romance in Winter

The fall of 1969 was when the Hilltop underwent changes that were meant to shake one to the core. It was a time of question and rebellion, an uneasy period in which long-standing rules were challenged and eventually swept aside in favor of new and different ideas. As much as possible, the slate of old beliefs would be wiped clean, and new graffiti would be chalked casually across the empty space.

The college campus was to experience vast remodeling, especially in its social structure. Quiet forces in student government were chopping at steel locks on closed doors. When the locks finally fell off, the campus was presented with its infant, the "open dorm." It was the single most revolutionary invention since the pill.

One particular senior wept at its unveiling. He lived on fourth floor Nilo, and his nickname was Mr. Underwear. As soon as he returned from his classes, he would strip down to his shorts and cavort around the dorm. No one ever saw him in any other clothes. Since "open dorm" meant women on the floor, some embarrassing moments were sure to follow unless he mended his ways. He never did; he attained celebrity status instead. A girl who could boast of actually seeing him was honored among her peers. The mere possibility of seeing Mr. Underwear would seduce any girl to go after fourth floor Nilo guys. Keeping my rotten luck intact, I had moved to third floor, with Don, for my sophomore year.

I have always been thankful that I had one year of restrictions, discipline, and asinine rules to follow. It made me appreciate the freedom when it came. Many younger students chose constant parties over study, and they flunked out at an early age.

Courting was as important as any course, and now there were plenty of opportunities to be alone with a girl. This painful fact didn't make it any easier to sit around and read in the dorm. However, love was just around the corner for me. First love is the only one that seems to last forever; at least, it never dies in one's memory. I was definitely dealt a knockout blow. I was so excited I didn't even try to analyze the feelings. I just enjoyed them.

Paul and Mike threw a party in early October. It was there that I was introduced to Jane Baker, a vivacious girl. She grew up in Minnesota and loved winter sports. A freshman, she was short, smart, and sexy. She shyly looked away from my open-mouthed stares several times that evening, and both of us knew it wouldn't be the last time we saw each other.

Our first official date was Halloween night. We saw a movie in town (I passed on the grape soda) and went for a walk. Our dating became more frequent as the weeks went by, although this was dating of a most informal nature. Without transportation, couples were restricted to the campus and the town. A cup of hot chocolate in the Cat was considered a regulation date.

Jane and I went on our first big date near the end of November. Doubling with Paul and his girlfriend Linda, we rode the student bus into nearby Cedar Rapids for a night on the town.

"You sure you don't want to see the Liza Minelli movie?" I asked Paul.

"Not when the Duke's gonna be on this screen," responded Paul.

"Well, we're going to see this movie," I hesitated. "You're sure that's okay, Jane?"

"Any film's okay with me," she smiled seductively.

This was the worst decision I could have made. Not only did the Liza Minelli movie have sex scenes, which made me uncomfortable, the John Wayne flick was great, and he went on to win an Academy Award for Best Actor.

After the shows, we all met at a local restaurant for a hamburger. I choked down the burger while I listened to Paul go on about the Duke's performance.

Jane had a wonderful time, and as far as she was concerned, the evening was a success. When I finally dropped her off at her dorm, our eyes met. Our good-night kiss ignited hidden fires which had never blazed before.

I walked around in pleasant shock for the next two weeks. I lived for the time spent with Jane. I saw her most nights after I finished studying, for an ice cream cone in the Cat. There were no two ways about it; we were falling in love.

Although the relationship was satisfying, I wanted a more intimate one. I hoped Jane would be willing to participate in a sharing partnership that would lend itself to experimentation in new activities; in other words, sex.

My background experience was fairly limited. I had never even seen a Playboy magazine until I was in college. I had only touched a girl's breast once, and that was by accident. As I reached to grab a handful of French fries from the plate of one of my high school dates, I brushed against her ample bosom with my hand. She giggled as I blushed and nearly fainted. That was the extent of my sex life thus far.

My room, 308, did not have the proper atmosphere for romance. The floor was tile except for two dirty rugs by the beds, and the walls were colored institutional beige. Even the dimmest lights in the room, the desk lamps, were bright enough to be used for the third degree, and the overhead fixture provided the equivalent of stage lighting. Don had stuck sports pictures and posters all over the place to give it the atmosphere of a locker room. The only thing it needed was stick-up slogans such as: "Show me a good loser and I'll show you a loser" or "Nice guys finish last." There was no television, no stereo, and no food or drink. There wasn't even a Monopoly game. The only thing I could offer Jane was myself. Somehow, I knew I could do better than that.

As I was returning from shopping in town on a cold December afternoon, the solution to my problems came running up behind me. It was my good friend Mike. We had become fast friends during our first year at school, and we counted on each other during times of crises.

"Hi, Michael. How're you doing?"

"Okay. I was just picking up some food in town. You like Oreos?"

"Love 'em," I said.

He reached into his shopping bag, broke open the sack of cookies, stuffed one into his mouth, and handed me a couple.

"Thanks," I said.

"Welcome. What's in your bag?"

"I bought a Monopoly game. I'm having Jane up to the room Friday night, and I want to have something to do."

"Oh, you sly dog," Mike chuckled. "I know what you're up to."

"Yeah. You guessed it," I admitted with a smile. "My room could use some shaping up, though. It sure doesn't look very romantic."

"No problem," said Mike. "'Tis the season to be jolly."

"Huh?"

"It's Christmas time, man. Let that spirit work for you. Christmas decorations is what you need. It'll give your room a whole new feeling."

"Yeah," I smiled. "I can see it now. Wreaths, holly, mistletoe, colored lights. I'll even get some of that pine spray to make the room smell like a Christmas tree."

"No, no," said Mike, shaking his head. "Don't use imitation junk. Let's get the real thing."

"A Christmas tree?"

"No, just the branches. We'll break them off trees out by the railroad tracks. We can put them in the window ledges and run blinking lights all through them. They'll give you the real beauty as well as the real scent. How's that sound?"

"Fantastic," I said. "Let's get on with it."

That night, we embarked on our mission under the silent winter canopy. The stars shone brightly in the dark blue sky, and the moon beams reflected a thousand crystals in the pure whiteness of the snow. The uneven path of our footprints followed us across the trek of land.

When we reached the railroad tracks, we buried ourselves in the hidden passageways which ran among the giant trees and went about our task of gathering branches. Once, we stopped our work to look out through a natural window framed by limbs. In the distance, the lights of the campus buildings shone serenely into the darkness.

"Boy, that's really beautiful," I said.

"It sure is," Mike agreed.

"I don't think I've ever seen the campus look so peaceful. And you notice how quiet it is out here? There's not a sound anywhere."

"That's what it's like out here," said Mike, who grew up in Iowa. "It's not like the big city, where the cars and trains run on forever. The country sleeps during the winter."

"It doesn't seem real to me. It makes me thankful I came to school here. And the great thing is we've got so much time left to appreciate all this. We'll be here for a long time."

Trudging over the snow-covered field where the baseball team would play its spring games, we expressed assurance that our college days would last forever. We covered our old footprints as we walked.

After the snow and ice had melted off the branches, leaving a pool of water and stems on the floor of the room, Mike and I decorated the window ledges with the evergreens and strung Christmas lights through them. With the lights blinking on and off, it was a marked improvement in atmosphere.

The following evening, Mike and I headed into town to buy some wreaths and mistletoe. A piercing wind cut through our winter coats. Main Street, which was the central route through the small business district, was brightened by the dangling, wind-blown lamps and ornaments that were draped on wires overhead. It was six-thirty and pitch dark save for the artificial lighting. The stores, which usually closed at five o'clock, were open to accommodate Christmas shoppers who worked during the day.

We chose the five and ten for our intended purchase. Mike wandered around aimlessly while I loaded my arms with some packaged wreaths and garland. I grabbed the small package of mistletoe as I walked toward the cash register. Minutes later, we pushed open the door and stepped out into the street. The cold wind whipped savagely at us. I transferred the big brown bag to my left arm and pulled my collar snugly around my exposed neck. "Man," I said, "is it ever cold. Let's get home fast."

"We've gotta go to Bob's supermarket yet."

Bob's supermarket was located all the way down a long, steep hill. The store was a good half-mile down the road on the corner of the intersection with the highway.

"What for?" I protested. "Why do you want to go all the way down there on a night like this?"

"So your love life will be complete."

"Huh?"

"We have to get the mistletoe."

"I got it already."

"What? They had it in there?"

"Sure." I reached down into the bag and pulled out the small package. "There you go, sweetie. Pucker up."

"My ass. This stuff's plastic."

"Well, of course it's plastic. What did you expect, rubber?"

"I know this is going to come as quite a shock to you, but there's such a thing as actual mistletoe. It grows in Europe. This is just a cheap American imitation. Bob has the official product."

"Is that a fact?" I was truly amazed. I never knew mistletoe was anything but a manufactured piece of decoration. I continued to argue with Mike that it was still too damn cold to walk the entire distance to Bob's.

Mike disagreed.

We walked backwards toward the highway to avoid the knife slashes from the wind, shouting unkind words with each tired step. It was a miracle we made it to the supermarket, because for each step forward, the current would push us back.

When we finally arrived, we joyously swung open the screen door of the archway. It was there that our journey ended. I have always been at a loss to discern why store owners leave on their neon signs long after they have locked up for the night. In the long run, it probably pissed off more of Bob's potential customers who, like us, vowed never to return.

After gathering strength by huddling in the unheated archway and furiously kicking Bob's pop machine, we began our return trip. I foolishly followed Mike through what he claimed was a shortcut to campus. It may have been shorter, but it was hardly less treacherous. The snow was knee deep. We plodded, stumbled, fell, got up, and plodded some more until we eventually reached the safety of our dorm.

Thawing out in our underwear, we watched a puddle form for the second consecutive night on the floor of my room. We wrung the final drops of water out of our soaked jeans, and I thought of how mothers yelled at little kids for such childlike stunts.

The final decorations were added to the room that night, and a green gel was placed over the ceiling light. The atmosphere was exciting and peaceful at the same time. I was confident Jane would love it.

Truly romantic evenings come seldom in one's life. I have always been thankful for that Friday night with Jane. We had a super time, talking and laughing with each other in the quiet, comfortable setting. I didn't feel rushed to try and start making out with her, because I was having too much fun just being with her.

I suddenly looked up at the clock and knew the night was over. I was very glad that the phrase "open dorm" had come to campus. People needed more time to get to know each other in private surroundings. Jane and I had done that tonight.

"It's almost twelve," I said. "I think I'd better walk you home."

"I had a lovely time tonight," said Jane as she put on her winter coat and gloves.

"So did I."

She headed toward the door, leaving her stocking cap on the chair. I picked it up and followed her across the room. She turned to face me, and I slipped the cap over her head and pulled it down against her ears. She smiled up at me. I smiled back.

"We're under the mistletoe," I said softly.

"It doesn't count," she said. "It's plastic."

"Give the city boy a break, will you? It's the best I could do."

We laughed and kissed each other. The mistletoe didn't know the difference.

Chapter 10 – "Ladies and Gentlemen . . ."

"Growth is the only evidence of life." I read that on a poster once. It didn't say who the author was, but I didn't care. It made sense. Posters were an important addition to almost everyone's room. They were used to add meaning to an otherwise senseless, blank space. Don preferred sports figures; I preferred rock-'n-roll heroes. There were Simon and Garfunkel, Bob Dylan, and the Beach Boys. But, most of all, there were the Beatles. John, Paul, George, and Ringo in glorious color.

I was working one morning when Mike came to put his tray on the breakdown line. "Hey! Paul McCartney's dead."

"What?"

"Yeah. He was in a car accident – back in 1966."

"What do you mean – back in 1966?"

"That's what I mean. They've been using a decoy ever since. It's all on their new album – and the rest of their albums from what I can gather."

There was a meeting in Paul's room that night. He really hated the Beatles, but since he was the only one who had a record player, we all went to town and purchased their new album "Abbey Road," and borrowed the other three albums – the "White Album," "Magical Mystery Tour," and "Sgt. Pepper."

It was all there.

Starting with the single "Strawberry Fields Forever," there was the cryptic ending which sounded like: "I buried Paul."

"Sgt. Pepper" was a graveyard scene, and a mirror placed over "LONELY HEARTS" came up with the date he died: "1ONEIX – HE DIE" - "On November 9 – He Die" with a diamond between "HE" and "DIE" pointing directly to Paul. The bass guitar lying next to the grave is placed in a left-handed position waiting for Paul to pick it up. And if that wasn't enough, the first half of "A Day in the Life" talks about his death.

"Magical Mystery Tour" features "I Am the Walrus," which ends with the death scene from "King Lear," which features such lines as: "bury my body," "O, untimely death," and "What, is he dead?"

The "White Album" has myriad clues. The first one is "Glass Onion," featuring John singing, "Now here's another clue for you all, the Walrus was Paul." The other clues are backward chants: "Paul's dead, miss him, miss him," and "Turn me on, dead man. Turn me on, dead man."

The best, and most conclusive, was the front cover of their newest album. "Abbey Road" shows the four Beatles walking across an intersection. But, wait. It's really a funeral procession. John, wearing all white, represents the clergy; Ringo, all in black, is an undertaker; George, following the group, is the gravedigger, and Paul, out of step with the others, is the corpse.

I have left out many clues, but the bulk is there. This rumor has fed on illusions through the decades and, even though everyone knows Paul is really alive, the Beatles were blamed for a hoax. It spread through college kids like crazy. We were one of the firsts to be playing the albums backward, looking for clues. We were the first to be deceived.

****

The theatre presented me with a chance to confuse myself more than was necessary. If a person acts for too many years, or takes it too seriously, he loses touch with the real person and becomes a collage of personalities. I had always enjoyed acting and saw it as an opportunity to assume the charm of a Robert Redford, the humor of a Woody Allen, and the dashing heroics of a John Wayne, all rolled up in one choice part. True to my own nature, I was usually cast as the policeman with two lines and no name.

I was never into the theatre. Not like the real theatre people were into it. I enjoyed it; that wasn't enough. It was not an extracurricular activity; it was a total commitment, a way of life. No one knew who the theatre people were. That's because no one ever visited them in their live-in quarters. No normal people went inside the theatre except to see a play, where they'd see the theatre people pretending to be characters other than themselves. Even on those rare occasions when the theatre people slipped silently out of their homes, they were not recognized by the other people on campus. They never stayed away long, returning unnoticed to blend into the walls like the clay people in the old Flash Gordon series.

It was a fact. The theatre people lived in the theatre for the theatre. If they weren't learning lines for a big part in a show, they were making costumes or painting sets for another show. Almost all their courses met informally in the Green room, which was the barren makeup room surrounded by olive-green walls. The tiny cubicle was highlighted by rows of naked white light bulbs reflecting off endless mirrors that had silently watched thousands of Jekyll and Hyde transformations.

Their leader was Guy Seneval. He was the chairman of the department and the person responsible for producing and directing the theatre's plays. Although most people didn't consider him to be the sweetest flower on the face of the earth, few could deny that he was a genius, one who hated his actors.

Guy designed his sets and lighting so that it was nearly impossible to see the performers. Every set was basic black with silver aluminum foil for trim. The lighting, which was never directly focused on the lead characters, was purple and orange. Audience members had to strain just to see the stage. He would have made a great undertaker.

****

I began my brief acting career during the second semester of my sophomore year when I signed up for Acting 105. The class met every TTS at 10:00 AM under the tutelage of Professor Chester. Every Saturday, a cutting from a play was performed by some of the approximately twenty members. The plays were directed by students in Chester's directing class, and the audience was made up of the remaining members of the acting class. Rehearsal time was usually three weeks.

After a few small parts, I was cast in a lead role for one of the funniest comedies ever written, Neil Simon's The Odd Couple. I was Felix Unger, and Paul was cast as Oscar Madison. The director was a senior named Steve Platson, who liked to scream viciously at his actors during rehearsal. He said if his actors feared him, then they would work for him and be in top mental and physical condition for the final show. It was a simple philosophy of dictatorship.

Paul and I wondered if Steve would torture us if we forgot our lines during the show. We decided he wasn't that tyrannical. So, we rehearsed nervously through the shouting and the stomping as Steve molded young actors into full-fledged stars.

The play was not being put on in the theatre itself, but down below in the Underground. This was the name given to the smaller, more intimate area used by the theatre for productions-in-the-round. The theatre people spoke knowingly in hushed tones of the Underground, where all the new, surrealistic plays were performed. In reality, it was the basement of the theatre, complete with unadorned cement walls and rusty ceiling pipes. But it didn't sound as well-meaning to call it the "basement," so the name was changed to impress the public.

Paul and I had no trouble adapting to our parts. We were type-cast. Paul was naturally boisterous, sloppy, and crude, whereas I was painfully neat and maddeningly meticulous. Friends left pillows strewn carelessly around my room just so they could watch me put them in their proper place with a final adjustment of a corner. Don complained more than once about missing clothing only to find it hung neatly in his closet or folded crisply in bureau drawers. Speaking frankly, I drove people nuts with my unrelenting passion for neatness. Felix would have been proud of me.

On the set, I swept, stacked, and sorted more than an English nanny. Scenes stopped suddenly as I dashed across the stage to retrieve a crumpled piece of paper on a table. Our director merely screamed obscenities at me. Finally, he hired a maid to thoroughly dust and vacuum the stage before the final show. He could've saved the money and let me do it.

Directors never worry about actors during a performance. I had always assumed that a director sweated out every line right along with his cast. Not so. The tech crew gives the director his severest ulcers. A show can be ruined by a technical mistake. When an actor in the wings misses his cue, the people on stage can cover for several minutes if necessary. But not with the tech crew.

Although our sound man was inexperienced, we weren't worried about him making any mistakes. The master tape recorder was hooked into the speaker system and issued only three sounds during the entire play: a doorbell ringing, a toilet flushing, and a dish crashing against a wall. Steve decided to have Paul (Oscar) throw a rubber plate full of mock linguini past my head into the kitchen area with the sound of the breaking dish to follow immediately after. I was not sure whether Steve did that to save himself a messy wall, or to insure against my abandoning the rest of the scene to clean it off with a religious fervor.

We worked like mad dogs during the last week. The night of the final dress rehearsal arrived suddenly. Steve gathered the whole cast beside him.

"Now, listen, I am only going to say this once," Steve began. "You're on your own. If you make any errors or forget any lines, you'll have to cover for yourselves. Understand?"

"What if the tech guy makes an error?" I asked.

Steve stared at me. "Well, that's not gonna happen."

Steve did keep his promise that night, too. At least until the chase scene. After I take pills in an attempted suicide – this is a comedy – I am chased around the room and dragged down into a chair by Oscar and his poker buddies. This worked without a hitch. In fact, it was one of the few scenes that Steve claimed was halfway decent. But, not that night.

"Aaaaaaaaah!" I screamed.

The front leg of the chair shot out, and I was immediately flung onto the floor. The unexpected fall caused the seven of us to burst out into uncontrollable laughter.

Steve was furious. "You morons! What if that happens tomorrow? Are you gonna laugh like a bunch of baboons. C'mon, comedy is serious business."

The following morning, I knew he was right when the butterflies began gnawing at my stomach. Consequently, I shared the three deadly fears of every stage actor: would I succumb to the common paranoia of forgetting a line, did they spell my name correctly in the program, and would the makeup ever come off?

The play was successful as far as the actors were concerned. Paul and I did a credible job, and we enjoyed the enthusiastic laughter and appreciative applause from the audience. I didn't mess up any of my lines, and the (new) chair held up. From that day on, I was an addict; the theatre was in my blood.

Unfortunately for our young sound man, he never overcame his own three deadly cues. When I rang the docrbell, we all had to wait. Finally, it rang. When I flushed the toilet, we all had to wait. Finally, it flushed. When Oscar threw the plate of linguini, we all had to wait. Finally, there was the sound of the dish breaking. The audience tittered. The response could have been worse. After all, it <u>was</u> a comedy, and – let's face it – you'd never see it in the movies.

****

My brother Tom was two years younger than I, and he was going to have to think about going to college. There was only one big problem: he loved his guitars and hated the thought of more schooling. Nonetheless, he was sent on a plane to investigate the Hilltop.

It was Friday, and I was forced to commit suicide because I'd just flunked, or so I thought, my economics test. I slammed open the door of my room.

"Okay, I flunked my econ test."

Don, who never got less than an A on any course, smiled. "Oh, I'm sure it's not that bad."

I dumped my Mason jar full of pencils on the floor. "Damn, it is that bad! How do I become a priest?"

"What?"

"Well, I've seen the priest on Sundays. He doesn't really work that hard."

"Well, we'll think about that tomorrow. You have to get Dennis and pick up your brother at the airport."

"Oh, yeah. I almost forgot."

I quickly forgot about the economics test and concentrated on getting my brother to campus. Let's put it this way. His interview with one of the administrators went not so well, especially when he was asked what he wanted to do with his future.

"Future?" my brother asked. "I just want to sit around and play my guitar." (Smart answer.)

It was clear he didn't see the Hilltop – or any other school of choice – as a feasible option. What he did think was a viable selection was to see a horror movie at one of our local drive-ins with Mike and Dennis. He was very proud to quote the line from the movie that he and Mike would repeat: "Swamp thing! Better watch out for the swamp thing!"

I put my brother back on the plane Monday morning. I went to economics class where I found I had received a B on my test. Some things were as they were meant to be.

Chapter 11 – Free Angela

The late sixties – a time of unrest for the United States. Many young people were looking for their inner selves, but most of us were not looking in the right place or with the right devotion. Individuals found themselves thrust into battle either for or against a given cause, of which there were too many to count. There was no middle ground. At one time, I went around with a group of activists shouting at people, "Free Angela!" It took me two weeks to figure out who Angela was.

The Vietnam War was hell – it was tearing the nation in half. Even when I was convinced that my involvement in peaceful anti-war demonstrations was a morally good thing, I was worried about being arrested. My radical left-wing friends told me it was an honor to serve time in the "pig pens," which was hippie language for jail. These same crusaders ran like hell at the sound of a police siren.

One thing was for certain. I was confused. All during sophomore year, I wasn't sure where I should take a stand. I didn't like the anti-war demonstrators very much. They'd preach non-violence and then pitch a brick through a window – or worse. Whereas the silent majority would cheer wildly at home as police clubbed innocent bystanders at peace rallies.

Then came Tricky Dicky's first-time-in-our-memories draft lottery. We all sat around the TV set in the lounge and waited for our draft numbers to be picked. I was 84; Dennis was 88. The only real pair of grunts waiting to be picked for active duty in Vietnam. Dennis put up his draft number with this message on the door to his room: "I'm number 88! Kiss my ass good-bye!"

The scene settled down and we were ready to be carted away to our summer homes – or jobs. Don finished up very early, said farewell to all of his friends, and was picked up. Halfway through our college career. What could go wrong?

April 30, 1970. President Nixon went on TV and talked about the Cambodian incursion. Wait a minute. Why attack Cambodia? Wasn't the war in Vietnam supposed to be coming to a close? Was Nixon lying? Student strikes took place all over the nation, from college campuses to high schools.

May 4, 1970. Four students at Kent State were shot and killed by members of the Ohio National Guard. Two were walking to class; the boy was a member of the ROTC. Nine more were wounded, one so bad he was paralyzed for life. Within less than two weeks, a song written by Neil Young for Crosby, Stills, Nash, and Young received air play on national radio – it was called simply "Ohio."

Anyone who was on a college campus was stunned. It didn't matter if a college person was for or against the Vietnam War; a new form of open warfare had been declared against all of us. President Nixon and Vice-President Agnew were the enemy, and their transgressions against the freedoms of ordinary people were clear to those who were not afraid to look. I was no longer afraid to look.

A few days after the Kent State murders, the campus was aroused one evening by students who were calling for an all-school meeting in the Chapel to decide whether we should take final exams or not. The reason was a protest against the killings. The time was to be spent in workshops to learn more about the War, the draft, and other related matters. The question was academic as finals were two days away from being finished. I pictured calling Don and telling him he had to come back to campus and refuse to take exams.

Campus history took place that night. It was a memorable evening that saw the entire student body together at the same time. No football game ever drew that size crowd. I decided early that I would vote to finish exams, because I knew that the world would not stop if we didn't hold finals as usual. Radical Ed Barkley made a radical-type speech telling the campus that a discussion of whether exams should be taken was bullshit when there was a War going on and innocent people were being killed. He was right for once. He would finish his college career at another – more liberal – university. The popular vote wasn't even close. Exams were finished, and we went home for the summer.

****

My summer job was the same as usual. I worked in an all-women's department, courtesy of Webbert Marking Systems. The women were amazed I was halfway through my career, and that I should "stick to it" or I'd end up working in a place like this for my whole life. I didn't think it sounded so bad. My boss (a male) would give me something to do, and I'd work on this no matter how long it took – three days for one thing, two weeks for another. It was simple. And, besides, the place was air-conditioned.

I was delighted to receive a letter from Jane twice a week. She'd share what she was doing, and, of course, I'd write her back. Until the week before we were supposed to return. Then, I received a letter I never expected. The gist of it was this:

"I'm not going to come back to be with you this semester. I'm going to stay in St. Paul and go to Morton College this fall –

maybe forever. My parents can't afford the Hilltop. I'm really SORRY. My heart is broken. What can I say? I'll always love you!!!

Love, Jane"

And that was it. My first big romance had come to a screeching end just when it was starting to bloom. I'd just have to wait and see what junior year held for me.

****

The following autumn saw the peace movement ready for action. Moratoriums were scheduled at regular intervals. I had learned all the familiar slogans of the non-violent marches for peace. These chants were organized like the rhythmic cheers one hears at sports events. "Go! Go! Go! Fight Win!" became "Hell no! We won't go!" And the traditional question-answer from the cheerleaders to the crowd was also included in the peacenik's handbook. "What do you want?" "Peace!" "When do you want it?" "Now!" was a favorite. Everyone had to come prepared to sing John Lennon's anti-war song "Give Peace a Chance," which took about fifteen seconds to memorize completely.

Besides chants and songs, we wore dove buttons which read, "Work For Peace." Underneath the slogan were the three dates of that fall's national moratorium. It looked bad. People should only work for peace on those three days? A true peacenik took a black magic marker and rubbed over the accusing dates on the button.

Petitions stating grievances against the War were constantly circulated around campus. When they were signed, they were mailed directly to the White House. Those people who signed them were probably classified in the FBI files under subversives. I was actually quite pleased that I was considered potentially dangerous by the government. It made me feel like John Hancock or Sam Adams or one of those other troublemakers who signed documents of protest. I wrote one letter to Adlai Stevenson III, who was our national Senator representing Illinois. I was surprised to get a letter from him in return stating that he, like me, was against the War and pledging Congress's help to cut funds for it.

The challenge of November came in the form of the second-in-command,

Spiro T. Agnew, who was scheduled to speak briefly at the Cedar Rapids airport. I got Dennis to go with me, and we set off earlier than expected.

"The place will be loaded with farmers and businessmen," Dennis stated.

"Yeah," I said, "we'll get to see what the silent majority looks like. You know, the strategy is simple. It wouldn't do us much good to try and get everyone to chant anti-war slogans at him. So, we decided to turn it into an old-time political rally. We will cheer like crazy for the old man, and then maybe all those people will decide that they don't want to vote for the same candidate as all those freaky college kids."

We arrived about a half-hour before the plane was scheduled to land. It was an awful day, combining the very best of a biting wind with a moderately heavy rainfall. We huddled against the cold in the giant airport hangar, where the podium and microphone were set-up under shelter from the rain. The acoustics were similar to being in a subway tunnel. The yelling backfired off the walls to create a crowd atmosphere that was noisier and livelier than it was.

Before long, the plane set down, the door swung open, and the steps were lowered. As Agnew made his way to the platform where a host of politicians and officials waited for him, the multitude cheered wildly. Our gang broke into the act with a kazoo-band rendition of the Mickey Mouse Club song. We were into it now. The special atmosphere of politics in America was in the air; that electric excitement of a live appearance that totally involved even the most casual observer. Vice-President Agnew was in the room, and like him or loathe him, it was a thrill to watch him.

I noticed the media first. The camera featuring the bright television lights pierced the air in the direction of the speaker as he stepped forward. Spiro's face was caked with makeup, and he looked artificial and doll-like. The Secret Service agents on either side of him and above him were a constant reminder to everyone present that his life could be snuffed out in a second.

Halfway through his speech, our plans were cast aside when pointed remarks by Spiro spurred us to action. "Peace Now!" was chanted over and over until the speech was interrupted. Agnew squinted against the lights at our faces in the crowd. The television camera swung briefly through our lives. Dennis held his sign up high. It read simply: "Spiro in 1984." When the noise died down, Spiro said with a smile, "At least the good farmers here in Iowa <u>grow</u> their grass!" Mark Twain couldn't have said it better.

****

"John Denver's coming!" said Don.

"John Denver? He's really good," I said. "What does he want to come to Iowa for? Wait a minute. He was here last year, wasn't he?"

"That's right. And the student board signed him up for another year. Now, we'll see if he honors his own signature."

He was signed up for a concert in March, and this was just about the greatest musician we'd ever had on campus. He'd had one hit single, and that was enough for us.

Now, rumors circulate on a college campus faster than any place. The number one rumor was that, now that he was a big star, he wouldn't show up and would let his lawyers handle the mess. Lawyers vs. the kids on the Hilltop – oh, right. We'd really win that one.

This was technically part of the convocation series – a long, dry spell of underachieving speakers on a Thursday morning that we were sworn to attend. You only had three misses, and you were ejected. Everyone was planning on attending the John Denver concert. It was free.

If you look up the famous speakers on the Hilltop, it was quite impressive. One of the first was Helen Keller and her mentor Anne Sullivan. Most recently was Martin Luther King. Another was Robert F. Kennedy. Before my time.

Well, John Denver showed, and he did not disappoint. True, he did crack year-old jokes about Iowa, but he was in a pleasant mood. He sang his one hit, "Take Me Home, Country Roads." And he bound up the audience with a spoken monologue called simply "The Box."

We were lucky. John Denver would go on to a fabulous career with many more hit singles and albums. He was recognized world-wide, and, I understood, took up flying.

Chapter 12 – The Strange Case of the College Individual

One of the most important relationships anyone has in college is that unique personal concept of one's own self. During my college years, it was not unusual for the average student to go through many periods of adjustments, resulting in both inner and outer changes. In an attempt to find themselves, some people went overboard. Every time I thought I was the strangest person on campus, I would take a look around. Some of the weirdos I saw helped convince me I wasn't so different after all.

Larry Gatner was one such individual for the psychology, or psychiatry, books. Poor Larry was never sure who he was; nor was anyone else.

We didn't know much about Larry, even by junior year. He was shy and kept to himself most of the time. But he was always the center of attention when he had a small group of friends from the dorm around him. Then he would entertain everyone with his genuinely good imitations, which included celebrities, politicians, and the Hilltop faculty members. Plus, his otherwise tasteless, salty humor: "Let's go for some pizza. I'll have leper scabs on mine."

He had entered school with the rest of us, but was only a first semester sophomore, having picked up barely enough credits in two years to advance himself beyond the freshman level.

He had a good excuse. He had been severely ill with mono during the spring semester of freshman year and never regained his academic touch. His roommate Bill told us Larry had more than likely been committed to a mental institution during his absence from school, although he had no concrete proof. College students have always fed on rumors like that, and, true or not, it soon became common knowledge that Larry was at least somewhat mentally disturbed. The fact that Bill kept tarantulas in their room as pets somehow did not alter his credibility as an accurate judge of unstable people.

Larry's biggest problem was trying to find a girl. This didn't make him any different than any of us. It was the way he went about finding one or, more appropriately, the way he didn't go about finding one, that made him unique.

When I first was reintroduced to him, Larry accused me of spending too much time with girls. (Where was he looking?) He didn't need a girl. Nobody did. Yet he constantly bemoaned the fact that he didn't have anybody to go out with on Friday and Saturday nights, when everyone on the floor had dates.

We suggested several nice girls whom Larry might take out, but he already had two in mind, Wendy and Kathy. He idolized both from afar. He sat daily at lunch and gazed longingly at Kathy's little boobs resting on her food tray as she made her way through the crowded dining room, flashing a smile at the table of football players as she bounced by. He stared at Wendy every MWF at 9:00 in Spanish 201, which was strangely enough the only class he ever expressed much interest in. But he viewed these girls as unattainable objects of desire and never attempted to call them or ask them out.

It wasn't long before Larry had his chance at a dream date. Driven almost mad by his constant talking about one or the other, his buddies were scheming to set him up with Wendy. If that didn't work, then Kathy. But that ended in near disaster late one evening when, urged on by a cheering mob which included almost everyone on third floor Nilo, Larry was dragged down the hall on his stomach toward the phone by two so-called buddies while a third dialed Wendy's number. (We had our only phones hung in the hall – no cell phones!)

Third floor rocked with laughter as Larry moaned, "No, please. Not now. Not tonight. I'll call her tomorrow. She won't be home tonight. She's probably studying. No! No!"

Luckily for Larry, Wendy wasn't home. Fearing another attack on his person, he somehow managed the nerve to call her and pleaded with her to go out with him. (That, itself, was implausible.) She couldn't go out with him for one simple reason: she was engaged. She had been engaged for a year to Corky Stone, campus super jock. Larry had been staring at her for months and never noticed the diamond ring on her left hand. Thus ended his quest for the wonderful Wendy.

The closest he came to being with Kathy was one Saturday night in the Union while we were enjoying our weekly steak dinner. A group of us had arrived early and were sitting by a corner window watching the dining room fill up around us. It was one of the nights where everyone just "scrambled" for their food.

The group all saw her coming. Larry, with his back to the crowd and his face buried in his dinner, never noticed the approaching visitor. She slid through the tables, gracefully making her way toward the one filled with girls next to ours. Larry sat quietly munching on a French fry, still unaware of the grand entrance that was being made by his inaccessible lover. We felt the tension build as she placed her tray down directly behind our soon-to-be-fallen friend. Mike leaned forward and whispered to Larry as he pointed out toward the dining hall, "There's Kathy."

"Where?" Larry shouted the word out as he spun around. She stared straight down at him, an amused smile pushing out her small cheeks and forming dimples at the corners of her mouth. Larry's eyes, frozen in terror, locked with hers.

Still smiling, she said to him, "Is there anything I can do for you, or do you always stare at strangers with your mouth open and the chewed-up food showing all over your tongue?"

The girls, as if on cue, laughed loudly. Larry never mentioned Kathy's name after that ill-fated evening.

Not long before the end of the first semester, the rumor grew that Larry would not be with us long. We had become increasingly aware of the fact that he hardly ever cracked a book. He was very vague about his courses and his possible grades, also. We weren't even sure he attended classes, except he did such great imitations of all his profs.

Bill told Don, Dennis, and me one December day that Larry was flunking out. "He never comes to bio or math anymore. Not even on test days. I guess he doesn't feel like taking the tests when he hasn't read any of the material. The only class he ever went to was Spanish, but stopped when he found out Wendy was engaged."

"You're kidding," I said, but we all realized Bill was telling the truth. Larry would be leaving school for good at Christmas. We all made a special effort to be nice to him, even though he became as surly as a bear as the weeks went by. He never once let on that he would not be back, and even continued the chicanery of discussing his classes as if he were still an integral part of them.

The night before he was scheduled to catch an early plane for home, Larry hadn't packed any of his belongings except for one suitcase. He asked Dennis and me to get up at 5:30 and take him to the airport.

We rose in time and trudged sleepily down to his room. Bill was asleep, and Larry was gone, never to be heard from again. A taxi had taken him and his belongings away from campus earlier that same morning. He had taken with him Richard Nixon, Hubert Humphrey, Ed Sullivan, and most of the profs on campus. Somewhere in that jumble of humanity, he had probably remembered to take the real Larry. I certainly hope he unpacked him when he got home.

****

We also lost some of our dearest friends during junior year. Don and I were in Room 327; next door were Arnie and Woody, who never made any noise. We were shocked to find out they were leaving at Christmas break. Arnie was going to a big university to study medicine; Woody was going to a music-centered college to study violin.

We were sad. Arnie was one of the best basketball players, and we would miss him on Saturday morning. Woody always studied, so we never saw him, except for dinner. But, every Sunday afternoon, he would come to our room to see how his team, the Kansas City Chiefs, was doing. It was funny. He never showed much emotion, but let those Chiefs start to lose, and brother, did he go mad.

We were happy that room was going to be empty. Not even a little noise to wake us at night. Until the college put two freshmen in that room, who liked to party every Friday and Saturday night. It was a long semester. But, as I said before, some students come to party and get kicked out. At the end of the semester, they were long gone. Bye-bye, goofballs.

Frank Soader was one of my best friends at school. But, he had become a theatre person, and he felt obliged to leave at the end of his junior year.

One night in March, we all went to the Amana Colonies, where we ate "family style." While there, Frank shared with everyone his dream for his directorial debut, a play he had written featuring "Hey Bulldog" by the Beatles as a theme song. I read it when we returned, and it was a masterpiece. I sure hope he got to put it on somewhere. I never saw Frank after he left.

I would have bet my marbles that I would continue to be best friends with my college buddies – Don, Dennis, Paul, Mike, Arnie, etc. We were b.f.f., weren't we? But, as long as God makes little green apples, time hurries on. We were doomed to be Christmas-card friends, and that's all. C'est la vie.

Chapter 13 – "You Can Always Study Tomorrow"

Dennis and I drove back to campus together in early September. It was an unusually quiet ride, considering the enthusiasm that had been shown during August to get back home and fire up for our senior year. As the car sped toward the Hilltop, we secretly struggled with our innermost fears, fully aware that the following May we would be out in the real world and responsible for making a living somehow. Whenever I thought about actually working for a living, I shuddered. Although we still had a long time to enjoy the many freedoms of college life, we were all aware that we would view each passing day of this last year with an added significance.

It was a year packed with so much fun, it's hard to remember ever opening a book. Don and I had all the luxuries of a bachelor pad in Room 323, a corner room away from the noise and bustle of the main traffic route through Nilo. Our third straight year together as roommates saw us well-equipped with a brand-new blue-green carpet, stereo, color television, and a food table in the corner that was always filled with such nourishing items as cookies, fruit pies, potato chips, and pretzels. The refrigerator in the late fall and winter was the window ledge. The cold temperature kept soda pop and beer colder than most indoor refrigerators, sometimes so cold that the liquid would freeze up inside the can. With temptations like these in one's own room it was no wonder that the year's favorite expression was, "You can always study tomorrow."

We believed that. Every time I tried to read by myself in my room, I would either fall asleep from having been out too late the night before, or turn on the stereo or the boob tube. If I was successfully accomplishing something, Mike or Paul or Dennis would bang on the door and yell, "We're going out. We know you're in there booking. This is senior year, remember? You can always study tomorrow."

Out meant virtually anywhere, including frequent trips to Cedar Rapids for food. Any food would do, from McDonald's to Shakey's, but the real treat was Leonardo's Pizzeria with their famous Stromboli sausage, which caused more than one unsuspecting newcomer to gulp a quick glass of ice water to quench the sudden fire in the mouth. Morning excursions for food ended up at Ole's Ham and Egger, where we would eat ourselves under the table with ample portions of pancakes, eggs, ham, and bacon, followed by hot apple pie. Staying on campus meant visiting the donut guy. (This included, by the way, our regular dining of twenty-one meals a week.) The male college student's appetite is legendary, and we were no exception to the rule.

It was easy to screw around first quarter. The second quarter meant student teaching for Mike, Dennis, and me, but the first quarter involved only a few boring education courses that met once or twice a week. There was hardly any homework, only liberal sessions about how charming all students were and how it was the teacher's job to motivate them to work. This left us plenty of free time to have fun.

Mike introduced me to the Corner. It was the local tavern that all the Hilltop students frequented after their twenty-first birthday. Mike seduced me into the Corner one night, and we ate and drank until we were full. Besides the pizzas, which were out of this world, the tacos were super, and every Wednesday night was free salted-in-the-shell peanut night. By the end of the semester, Mike and I were habitual visitors to the Corner, and I really enjoyed that extra "snack" after dinner.

Similar to many small college bars, the Corner was a dive. The booths featured wooden benches and tables covered with graffiti which, when originally written, delighted some moron who just had to let the world know that a rival social group or his former girlfriend or the school, in general, "sucked." The walls were early American cement with cracks and holes. The floor was tiled yellow many years before, but was now an off-brown hue. These bad characteristics combined to give the place what is referred to as "atmosphere," which is college language for a dive. It did belong to the students, however. Townies only went there in the day. At night, it was packed with kids, sometimes so full that one could hardly get in the door. All in all, it was a great place to talk and get to know people. The beer was only fifty cents, and the pizzas were a buck twenty-five. I never regretted a night spent there. Whenever I expressed some little guilt about wasting time and money, someone would always be right there to say, "You can always study tomorrow."

Mike had also introduced me to some freshmen, who were to help me later in the year, although I didn't know it at the time. The three massive bodies were known as Panda, Pemby, and Bucko, all of whom weighed over two hundred pounds. I never asked where they got the weird nicknames. Their little friend, whom they referred to as Storkum Crevitz, was too small to hang around with this group. He was an artist. Together they made a strange foursome. For fun, the three big guys liked to toss little Stork around the room, or take turns jumping up and down on him to see who could make him scream the loudest. In public, they were the nicest people ever. It was only in private that they would take their aggressions out on poor little Stork.

One afternoon, to celebrate Bucko's birthday, they all decided to go into Cedar Rapids and "break-the-bank" at Shakey's all-you-can-eat luncheon. Mike convinced me, "You can always study tomorrow." So, we went. I don't know where Stork was. He was probably in the infirmary recovering from bruised ribs or multiple lacerations.

My guess is that no five people anywhere in the world have ever eaten a bigger lunch. I would not have been surprised if Shakey's cancelled their special after we had staggered out later that same afternoon. I can still see the manager's face as he first set eyes on the build of the five human beings.

"I'll have pizza number three," said Mike. "I don't know if I'll make it or not."

I had already stopped at pizza number two. Panda, Pemby, and Bucko raced to a hard-fought finish, Bucko being the winner with pizza number four. All of it, totaling thirty-two pieces of cheese pizzas.

Bucko washed down his last pizza with a huge gulp of a "green monster," a lime drink with a similarity to Alka-Seltzer in one important respect. It caused one to belch, thus clearing the way for more pizza.

"Buuuuurp." Bucko leaned back in his chair. "Oh, that was fine. Supposing we do that every lunch."

I was struggling just to keep two pizzas down; I couldn't imagine what Bucko's stomach was like with four pizzas in his gut.

As we took turns visiting the john the following day, making it hard to get any studying done, we were reminded of the following saying, "You can always study tomorrow."

****

As the fall months raced past, I enjoyed more and more my last year with the soccer team. In my four years on the Hilltop, soccer had moved from a club to a varsity sport. This entitled us to all the luxuries of the other team sports, such as the pre-game meal consisting of steak and eggs and pounds of honey toast for energy, and real-live buses for road trips to away games. Once, several years before, we had been forced to ride in a rented mini-bus. It had turned out to be a less-than-comfortable ride with our knees planted in our foreheads. As a consequence, our style of play had been somewhat "cramped."

Another gift made available to us through athletic department funding was new uniforms complete with warm-up pants and jackets. They were fashionable white fur, an embarrassment in any weather. They did turn out to be a blessing in cold weather, however, and we learned to ignore comments on the road like, "Hey, Commodore, how do you get to the North Pole?"

The only problem with the warm-up pants was the elastic around the waist. We found out the hard way that if we didn't clear it completely before we pulled the pants off, it would take one's shorts off right with the pants. I vowed it would never happen to me.

One home game, I was occupying my usual position on the bench. Suddenly, the coach tapped me on the shoulder and said, "Warm up. You're going in."

I was shocked. The game was only ten minutes old. I stood up quickly, raced over to a grassy area in front of the home fans, who had seen me get up and had started shouting encouragement, and pulled off my warm-up pants. As I was bending over to pull the pants over my cleats, I felt the cool October breeze on my moon, which was now fully exposed to the cheering crowd. They all started singing "Moon River." It had happened to me.

November 6, 1971. It was a sunny Saturday with the blue sky spotted with fluffy white clouds. Looking out a window, one would assume it was fairly warm. Actually, it was 9 degrees with a wind-chill factor close to -30 degrees. The icy wind raged at about 50 miles per hour. Our last game of the season was scheduled for that afternoon against our bitter rivals from Koxen College. It was a rivalry like the Bears-Packers. Since I had been on the Hilltop, they had beaten us twice each year, and had trounced us earlier that same year 5-1. Add two more defeats before my freshman year, and the grand total was 0-9. Our school had never beaten Koxen. A victory against them would take the Conference Championship away from them.

I was slated to start the final game. Yelling and hollering encouragement at each other as we did our warm-up exercises, we fought off the desire to run and hide from the cruel cold that battered our frozen bodies unmercifully. We wanted to beat Koxen more than anything else in the world that day, and we were all praying that our dreams would come true for us this one last time together. Then, we could all look back someday and know it had all been worth it – just once.

As the last game of my life began, I looked down at my legs. My knee socks were blue, my pants were white, and my legs were red from the cold. It matched my hat, a red, white, and blue stocking cap. I smiled. We couldn't lose. These were American colors. Long live Valley Forge.

Midway through the first half, I centered the ball to Francis Chong. His massive leg exploded, and he scored. I assisted the first goal. Actually, it was not that hard – the wind was at our backs. We scored another goal, and we waited for the onslaught from Koxen the second half.

We lined four fullbacks in front of the goal, as they powdered our goal. Twice, our star center from Africa dribbled the ball the length of the field and scored. It was over. The final score was 4-0. A shutout!

After the on-the-field celebration, we headed for free milk shakes in the Cat. As I walked across the barren brown grass, clutching an uneaten half-time orange in my near frozen fingers, memories of my involvement with this sport and the people who had touched my life flashed through my mind. My worn and broken cleats had carried me into competition for the last time. Looking down at my dust-covered shoes, I noticed every mark and tear. I reached down and grabbed a lost pen off the hard turf and paused momentarily. It must have been recently discarded, for it wrote right away. I scrawled across the side of the orange, "Victory Orange. 4-0 vs. Koxen. Nov. 6, 1971."

Although the orange eventually dried up inside, the writing remained legible, and the smaller piece of fruit is an interesting keepsake. It is preserved as hard as a rock with a light feeling and a rattle of seeds from within. As I looked back at the empty field with its solitary goals at each end, the orange still felt full and heavy in my hand, but there was a hollowness somewhere deep inside my own tired body.

Chapter 14 – The Other Side of the Desk

Walking briskly into the face of the sun, I was painfully aware I was beginning a new segment of my life, one that could not be taken lightly. It was a demanding, challenging, and very frightening world I was about to enter. The sweat began to break out in the hidden corners of my new suit. Passing by the front of Gordon Hall, I thought of the President's Reception and my first college date with Eunice. I had sweated then, too. But this time the sweat was more serious. I was about to begin my student teaching.

I walked rapidly through the center of town, the stillness of the surrounding shops a silent tribute to the early morning rays of the sun, which baked the east sides of the worn structures. I found it amusing that the Corner was one of the only buildings with an open door. Who'd want a drink at this time of the morning? After careful consideration, I continued on toward my destination.

I paused briefly in front of the brick building at the end of Main Street. Gazing at the non-air-conditioned high school, I took a deep breath and entered the ancient edifice through the double wooden doors. Oh, man, was it hot inside. After today, I would have a different point of view of education. My assigned seat was on the other side of the desk.

"Mrs. Rite, I'm Sean McKay, your new student teacher," I said to the grey-headed woman with glasses who was propped up behind the mountain of books and papers that was her desk.

"Oh, Sean, how good to see you," she said, a warm smile covering her weathered, tired face. That smile was destined to cheer me up whenever the trials of teaching started to depress me. During the next two months, I would learn a great deal from her about life as well as teaching. She was a talented woman, and I was lucky to be under her guiding hand. I liked her from that very moment she first welcomed me to her classroom.

"I'm so very happy that you'll be working with me," she continued. She was standing now and moved slowly around the desk to shake my hand.

"I'm looking forward to it," I said, smiling nervously as I fought down the fear rising within me.

Mrs. Rite shook my hand, then continued walking over to open the back windows. As she did so, I noticed the distinct limp in her stride. "I had polio when I was younger," she said, interrupting my thoughts. "It slowed me down quite a bit at first. Now it only bothers me going up and down stairs."

She returned to her cluttered desk and gestured toward an empty chair. I sat down. Almost immediately, I noticed why she looked shorter when standing. Her desk seat was a throne, a tall, wooden, straight-backed chair crowned with a Webster Dictionary for added elevation. She was seated high above the surrounding disaster on her desktop with a good vantage point of all corners of the large classroom.

"I find it worthwhile to keep the dictionary under me," she began, once again taking the thoughts from my head. "It gives me a splendid view of everyone in the room without cleaning off my desktop, which is in its normal state of chaos. It also keeps me in a position of power without standing. It's a good idea to remind the students every now and then who is in command. They have frequent memory failures and tend to take advantage if you are not firm with them."

I allowed my gaze to drift slowly around the room as she spoke. Instead of the traditional desks found in most high school classrooms, the furniture was composed of cushioned chairs and couches arranged in a semi-circle around a large, open area in front of the teacher's desk. I was amazed to learn from her that she had been using this liberal arrangement for several years.

"It took some strenuous pushing on my part to convince our principal it was a better way to conduct a class with the students all facing each other. It really does help them relate to their fellow classmates, their peers, about a variety of subjects. Expressing themselves in full view of their friends and learning to listen is a big part of growing up, I believe.

"You must help them grow and mature, Sean. That is what every high school teacher must be willing to do. There is no set system for that, no pat answers. Each teacher must use whatever gifts the Lord has given him to the very best of his ability, to make his students aware that maturity is the first step toward education."

Listening to Mrs. Rite, I realized I had a very large and serious assignment ahead of me. As students began to fill the halls outside the room, I knew the time was drawing near when I would begin my own education. All the courses on history, philosophy, and methods of education wouldn't help me much now. I would be working with real students, each one a unique and special person.

"The students will be coming in soon," said Mrs. Rite. "You relax for a few days, and we'll work you into the master position after you feel more comfortable with the surroundings. . . and the students."

I swallowed nervously and smiled weakly at Mrs. Rite. She smiled back kindly and confidently. I think she had more faith in me than I did. She had seen our breed before and knew we would all survive the ordeal. After I took over the reins of leadership, there must have been times when I shook that ironclad confidence of hers.

My transition into the main role went somewhat awkwardly. On my third day of observation, when only three minutes remained in the school day, an unexpected phone call pulled Mrs. Rite from the classroom. As she walked out, she turned calmly to me and said, "Mr. McKay, please take over the class for the remainder of the period, won't you?"

No, I won't, I thought. Sweat broke out on my temples as I rose to face the class. They knew who I was and why I was there, as I had been introduced by Mrs. Rite two days earlier. However, one second of silence followed the closing of the door. Then, a crescendo arose from the students, who began to talk to each other, completely oblivious to my presence in the room.

I tried to keep Mrs. Rite's lesson going with questions, but their answers were distracted by the general noise in the room. My mild requests for silence fell futilely short of their intended mark.

The bell saved me from more than a minimum amount of embarrassment. But it was enough. I had learned my first lesson. Never assume you have the student's respect until you have earned it. At the time, I could only think of illegal ways to get it. Since whips and blow torches weren't allowed in school, I would have to lay down the law without their assistance. Tomorrow they would listen to me. I had sworn revenge.

The next day I was prepared. I informed Mrs. Rite that I was ready to assume full responsibility of her sophomore speech classes. There were only seventy-five sophomores, and all of them had to pass the basic speech requirement. So, Mrs. Rite turned her second-, third-, and seventh-hour classes over to me.

I warmed up on the morning classes. I calmly and firmly laid down the rules and requirements for the next two months, explaining to the students that I had the final decision on their grades for the second quarter of the school year. Both classes were very responsive and impressed me with their cooperation.

Then came seventh-hour, a class full of demon boys. Unlike the previous day, I stood before them and demanded their undivided attention. It worked. I could tell that many of the students in this notoriously wild group would not give me trouble. Seventh-hour was always a little noisier than the morning classes, but it was basically made up of good, though sometimes misguided, youths. There was one notable exception, however.

Billy Hardell was the boy's name. He had an interesting face highlighted by large blue eyes which jumped wildly from side to side, giving the impression that he was always moving, even when he was sitting still. His flat nose and chin gave the bottom portion of his face a pushed-in look, which was broken only by the silver braces that shined out at the world with his frequent sardonic smiles. His matted brown hair and careless, sloppy clothes fit Billy's personality well. He was restless and curious, like a caged tiger, and he talked at an amazingly rapid rate, slurring and spitting as he rambled on about whatever went racing through his disorganized mind. He was the Achilles' heel of my student teaching days, and he made me thankful for weekends.

Billy was responsible for organizing many devious tricks that the class played on me, ranging from hiding the chalk to having all the students cough at the same time. During the second week of the quarter, he was the ringleader for one of the oldest pranks in the book. School was dismissed for the day at three o'clock. At five minutes to three, Billy shouted, "Look, Mr. McKay. The clock's stopped."

Many of the students began yelling that school was over, because the clock had been stopped for at least five minutes. Billy was bouncing excitedly up and down in his chair like a wild bull, a fiendish grin plastered on his face. Stupidly, I dismissed the class without thinking. It was two minutes too soon. They ran screaming out into the deserted, quiet hall. Unfortunately for me, just as they did so, the principal rounded the corner.

Mr. Winslow made a good high school principal. He was a large man with a round, bald head and a bass voice. When he spoke, his dark eyes commanded the attention of the listener. All of the students and most of the teachers feared him like the plague.

He walked purposefully down the hallway to my room, his massive frame blocking the entire doorway as he paused before entering. He looked briefly in my direction, then walked over to the wall where the clock hung motionless. Reaching down behind the chair, he retrieved the black electrical cord. Holding the unattached end in the air for my benefit, he said, "Sometimes these cords become unplugged very easily. Especially when Billy Hardell is in the classroom."

These and other practical jokes kept Billy and his seventh-hour buddies thriving. A hard core of five boys made up the elite group of troublemakers. I constantly kept Billy and his friends after school where they begged to be released, swearing they would never cause mischief again. The following day, they'd start disrupting the classroom almost immediately.

One Friday in early December, I evened the score with Billy Hardell once and for all. The sun was shining brightly outside, and the unusually warm temperature had melted away most of the snow. I was looking forward to a beautiful weekend as I headed toward my last class.

Mike Smith, who was student teaching in the music department, had waited behind at my request so we could walk home together. He had no seventh-hour class. Sitting patiently on a tall stool behind my desk, he watched as students charged noisily into the room.

Billy screamed as he entered, "Hey, hey! It's McGay-McKay!"

What a little jerk. I would be happy when this class was over. The students were working on a final project for Mrs. Rite, and I had to help them individually. I circulated around the room, giving guidance to those who needed it. As I was talking to some girls, Billy started goofing around with his buddies at a table behind me. I discovered that he quickly shut up when Mike stared a hole through him.

As I walked back to my desk, an excited Billy Hardell stopped me. Grabbing my arm, he babbled rapidly, "Mr. McKay! Mr. McKay! Who is that man? Who is that man?"

Looking over at Mike and for the first time seeing the severe stare he directed at Billy, I fought back an impulse to break out laughing. I had him now. Leaning closer to Billy, I said in a low tone, "Oh, that's Mr. Smith. He teaches in the city of Chicago in one of the bad schools with lots of troublemakers. He's a discipline teacher. His special job is taking care of bad students. He uses certain methods of punishment that are too cruel to talk about in public."

I thought Billy's round eyes were going to pop out of his head. His face was growing steadily paler, and his nervous little hands clutched my sleeve. The spit flew out of his mouth as he said, "Well, what's he looking at me like that for? I didn't do nothing wrong, Mr. McKay. I didn't do nothing wrong."

Almost splitting a gut inside, I said sternly, "That's right. It's Mr. McKay. I bet your tongue slipped when you came into class today. Isn't that right, Billy?"

He nodded passively.

"And you better not do anything wrong from now on. He's going to work at this school now. He's just looking around for some misbehaving students – to punish."

It was a mean trick to play on a student. But, Billy never caused any more trouble. In fact, I'm not sure he breathed the rest of the period.

Chapter 15 – My Favorite Teachers

Every college or university has its eccentric professors, teachers who are talked about by students for many years after graduation. The Hilltop was no exception. I had finished my student teaching, and it was very easy to tell them apart. Students signed up for their courses just so they could witness their doings in person.

Every department had at least one or two questionable cases. Professor Trumen, in science, was responsible for conducting unorthodox experiments at night. He worked at night because he was too busy playing football all day. He said he was trying to discover a new chemical, but we thought he was more than likely mixing elements in the hope of creating a low-calorie beer.

In math, there was the Duck and the Bismarck. The Duck was about sixty-five years old and put the book together that was taught to freshmen in "dumb-dumb" math. Paul, Dennis, and I had the Bismarck freshman year. The class would become lost during her lectures, which was no surprise in itself. Whenever she noticed the blank stares, she would remark that there seemed to be a wall between us. Then, she would burst out laughing, bouncing her ample backside up against the wall. At times such as these, we knew she wouldn't last long in the sane world. After grading our tests, she felt the same about us.

Professor Handly, in the economics department, was a nice young man with a Southern accent. His peculiar habit was his fondness for cigars. (Yes, professors smoked in class - mostly cigarettes.) He would produce a wrapped cigar from his coat pocket at the start of each of his classes. After fondling it for about ten minutes, he would remove the cellophane and pass the exposed object under his nose, breathing deeply and sighing, "Aaaaah."

Then, he would rotate the cigar carefully in his fingertips as he lectured, pausing to use it as a pointer when asking a direct question of a particular student. Finally, he would begin to roll one end around in his mouth while listening to the response. After the cigar was thoroughly soaked, he would light it.

The entire process took approximately one half-hour. The last twenty minutes of class were a noise fest with students breaking out in coughing fits. The smoke blanketed the air, as more than one student felt dizzy. Finally, we could take it no more. One classmate would bravely ask, "Professor Handly, could I please open a window?"

"If you must."

The sick-to-his-stomach student would get up, walk gingerly toward the window, and thrust it open. We inhaled the cold winter air, and it revived the class slowly.

Whereas some of the professors fit the mold of madness by small idiosyncrasies that were repeated day after day, others simply did the unexpected too often to be regarded as sane. The art department's own Professor Willy, or Weird Willy as he was known to the entire student body, was such an individual. If there was any doubt about the mental stability of some of the other faculty members, there was no doubt in anyone's mind about Willy. He was nuts. He once posed nude while holding a large duck in his arms for a painting by one of his female honor students. Another time, he wore a large, tin suit around campus for a week in protest against the computerized world that, according to Willy, was turning people into robots. He stopped wearing it shortly after some of his own art students erected a large green sign with a flashing arrow pointing toward the president's house on the hill. The sign read: "This Way to Oz."

Weird Willy's most famous act of madness was an art concert he held for any interested participants. Naturally, only his own students attended. The entire art gallery, floor and walls, was covered for the occasion with white drop cloths. In the middle of the hall was a large piano. As students entered, Willy made them don white coveralls. The only normal person there, the reporter/photographer for the school paper, stood in contempt as Weird Willy splashed his own white garment with chicken blood to begin the show. The art students applauded wildly. Next, he dumped an entire bucket of blood over his hair. With blood dripping off the ends of his black mustache, he grinned and said, "Now for my art concert."

Willy sat down at the piano and began to play. He started out playing nice, melodic little tunes, but he gradually shifted to heavier, louder, more somber numbers. Finally, he started pounding the keys with his fists. Screaming and swearing at the piano, Weird Willy grabbed an ax from under his robe and began to chop at the defenseless instrument. The blade split the smooth wood, sending chunks sailing into the air. Again and again, the ax fell to the sound of cheering encouragement from the art students. One of the legs finally cracked through, driving the piano to the floor. The blood-soaked Willy, teeth exposed in a werewolf grin, jumped on the piano and strangled the last remaining wires with his bare hands. Standing slowly, he turned to the now silent crowd of onlookers and said quietly, "It is over. The enemy is dead. I have conquered my own hatred and fear of death."

After a moment of silence for the deceased, handouts were distributed among the audience, each student receiving two paper cups filled with chicken blood. Willy told them they must not be afraid to show man's natural hatred for his fellow man. They were to attack by splashing blood on each other and shouting, thus working out all their inner hostilities.

So, they began. "I hate you," they screamed, throwing blood on one another, turning the white outfits a dark pink shade. All the while, Willy sat laughing in the middle of the piano ruins. The photographer for the paper snapped some good shots before some half-crazed girl turned on him and covered his lens with chicken blood. Fearing that Weird Willy might decide to use him for his next demonstration, the reporter made a hasty exit.

When the story and the corresponding photos appeared in the school paper the following week, normal students would veer suddenly if they saw Weird Willy heading toward them. It was the end of the '60's, but they weren't going to take any chances. I mean, the ax could have been hidden under his coat.

Professor Shackle, in English, was only one of several strange people in that department. The others, some of whom videotaped their lectures so as not to waste valuable political campaign time, were dismissed after only a couple of years. A once brilliant lecturer, Professor Shackle was now in his late seventies, but rumor placed his age at closer to ninety-nine. He was a very kind person who would have been great at his job had he sat on a park bench and fed popcorn to the pigeons. As a college professor, he simply didn't have it anymore. If he had been a baseball player, the expansion draft would have passed him by.

Thirty students signed up for his Shakespeare class. Age was constantly playing tricks with Shackle's mind, and he switched character's names from one play to the next. He had Macbeth and Hamlet mixed-up so badly, he had to stop and ask the class which play we were studying. And while reviewing the characters from A Midsummer Night's Dream, he called Puck by a similar name. It was the only time the class laughed together the entire semester.

Unfortunately, it was quite often that we napped together. It was not unusual for students to pop No-Doze before coming to class. Shackle's voice never varied in tone, pitch, or any other speech quality. Seated students were alternately sleeping, daydreaming, doodling, or writing letters to parents. No one listened; no one cared.

Professor Shackle brought in a tape one day while we were studying Hamlet. It was a recording of the play's dialogue. At last, some actors reading the lines – now we would be able to pay attention. Shackle started the tape, smiling at us, and sat down in front of the class. He was wearing a beige-colored shirt with no buttons and no collar. It was tucked into a pair of gray slacks. We always called it a nightgown, because that's what it looked like.

As the tape hummed on, Shackle's head began to droop. Before long, his chin rested squarely on his chest, his oval head pointing directly at us. His deep, regular breathing indicated an obvious pattern. Professor Shackle, the teacher, was sound asleep. None of us could believe it. We had seen students fall asleep in class before, but never a teacher. I woke up Dennis beside me and pointed at the now snoring Shackle.

Finally, with the whole class attentively watching him for the first time, Shackle snored loudly, jerked his head up quickly, and froze in sudden realization of the situation. Composing himself, he listened to the tape for a minute. Then, he slowly rose, walked to the desk, and turned off the tape. He asked us a question about a part of the play that had just been reenacted on the recording. It was a last-ditch effort to convince his class that he had been fully awake and a captive listener. Like his lectures, it fell fall short of its intended mark.

The education department had the gold-medal winner for weirdness, Professor Jay. If Handly was peculiar, and Willy was looney, then this woman must have climbed out of a banana tree. She stood about five feet high and was built like a bottle of beer. Her fireplug figure was always adorned with flowing jungle garments, which she brought back from her frequent visits to Africa. Her buoyant laugh could be heard echoing away over the countryside.

In class, she was a delight to listen to. Her lectures were spontaneous and joyful, and her stories were colorful. She called students by their surnames, prefacing each one with a Mr. or Miss. She had a difficult time learning mine and would continually address me as "Mr. McShay." After each mistake, she would babble loudly, "Oh, Mr. McKay, I am so sorry. I really am. I don't know what's wrong with me. I promise I shall be more careful next time, Mr. McShay."

As strange as Professor Jay was, her dog brought out the absolute Zulu in her. She lived alone in a nice house behind one of the girl's dorms. It was rumored that she had married once a long time ago, but was now divorced. Her only companion was her dog, Cactus.

Never had a more appropriate name been bestowed upon any living creature. This small, grey dog was covered with short, stringy hair that stuck out in all directions. When he stood up on his hind legs to beg for food, he really did resemble the desert plant after which he was named. No one ever demonstrated a great desire to reach down and pet him as he made his way across campus on his stubby legs.

This dog's home was his castle, however. Professor Jay saw to that. Cactus had his own bedroom with a little doggy bed, doggy dresser, and a wardrobe of the latest doggy fashions to wear on his strolls about town. At dog's-eye level were pictures of famous dogs such as Rin-Tin-Tin and Lassie.

I had heard about Cactus from Mike, who had taken a class from Professor Jay when we were sophomores. At the end of the semester, all her students, including Mike, were invited to her house for a pancake brunch. Everyone sat crossed-legged on the floor while they ate. Halfway through the meal, Cactus sauntered across the floor. Professor Jay laughed at the dog's antics as he stepped on people's pancakes. Everything Cactus ever did was funny to her. She probably would have laughed if he peed in the syrup.

Dennis and I took Professor Jay during our junior year for "Kiddie Psych." Every education major had to have a child psychology course before he could go into the teaching field. It was an interesting course for the most part, and we never fell asleep in class.

At the end of the year, we were invited to her home. Since it was a beautiful spring morning, we reviewed for the final exam in her backyard. We munched on chocolate chip cookies and brownies, and drank her homemade cider, which was spiked or left over from last fall, or both.

Cactus spent the whole time walking slowly back and forth on the brick ledge that ran at eye level to us. Suddenly, the dog's stomach started to growl, and he began to make grunting noises from his mouth. These were not to be mistaken for woofs or barks; they were grunts brought on by gas pains or acid indigestion. Professor Jay's face lit up like a beacon in a fog, and she squealed delightedly, "Listen, children, Cactus is going to lecture. Do you hear that, children? Cactus says that Dewey's philosophy is the only correct one, because it achieves the proper balance between the student and the teacher, and most suitably recognizes the teacher's guiding hand in the free learning experience."

Here we were, stuck like glue, a group of college students listening to a dog with an upset stomach. We would have ran away screaming, but finals were yet to come. We silently vowed to stick it out until the end, which was near at hand. Professor Jay rambled on for five additional minutes, smiling and calling us her children, which was somewhat disturbing. She summed up Cactus's speech and commented on a few significant highlights.

After his brief address, Cactus moved carefully among us, probably anticipating an autograph request from one of us peasants. He suddenly jumped up on my leg and barked; he was after my chocolate chip cookie.

As I broke off a corner of the cookie, I heard Professor Jay say, "Oh, no, Mr. McShay. Sorry, Mr. McKay. Cactus likes you, I can tell. You should be honored that he wants you to share your cookie with him. He doesn't like to be fed that way. No, no. Give him a bite right from the cookie. First you take a bite, then he takes a bite. Then you take a bite, then he takes a bite. That's what real sharing among friends is all about."

I thought I would be sick. I wouldn't even let my little brother drink from my pop bottle when we were growing up. No way was I going to let this mutt infect me with some kind of hoof and mouth disease. I gave him the whole cookie, saying I was too full to eat the rest of it. But I knew the atmosphere was getting to me. As I watched Cactus gobble up the remains of the cookie, I caught myself wondering what his after-dinner speech would be.

Chapter 16 – On with the Show

Winter hit hard that last year. Along with the usual heavy snowfall, there were three or four different ice storms. As beautiful as these were, especially when the morning sun reflected off the silver-coated branches, they were extremely hazardous to Hilltop life. All campus pathways led either up or down, and many were slanted at a dangerous angle. This made walking a feat in itself, and few did not take an occasional fall that featured octopus arms and legs flying recklessly in all directions before that jarring crunch upon impact with the frozen ground.

Mike was the only person I knew who never fell. Oh, he went up in the air the same as everyone else. It's just that he had a remarkable cat-like ability to twist his legs under him, so he could land on his feet rather than on his head. When I went up, my feet stayed above my head for the entire downward journey.

After a month of January blizzards, we were tired of winter and eagerly anticipated the coming of spring. But at the same time, we were all painfully aware that it would be the last spring of our college careers. We were in the stretch drive; the end was definitely in sight. If you've never lived through that, you have no idea what nervousness it inspires. I wanted to accomplish one worthwhile event while I was still in school. My grades were good, and my social life was active enough, but something was missing. I needed a personal achievement above and beyond the normal.

I had written a play during my sophomore year and wanted very much to direct it as a public performance in late

February. For a short time, I had my foot in the door, but it was slammed shut. Good old Guy Seneval decided that another student production would play in the theatre at that time, but said I could have the Underworld for the first week in March. My explanation that the play was a family oriented, three-act comedy and not suited for the Underworld did not move him. Consequently, I had three alternatives: I could produce my play in the Underworld, I could forget the whole thing, or I could try to get permission from the administration to use the Chapel for the show.

I decided to play the highest odds; I went for the Chapel. There had been shows in the Chapel for many years throughout the early 1900's. The acoustics were not the best, however, and all theatre productions gratefully shifted to the new building when it was finished in the late '30's. For the record, the first show starred Professor Chester, then a student, in a William Shakespeare play. During my junior year, one student production was put on in the Chapel, but after a stained-glass window was accidently broken during a rehearsal, the administration barred the doors against all future theatre shows.

I went to the wrong man immediately, the second-in-charge of the college, Le Grand Charles. Had I talked with him, he would have instructed me to abandon my wild scheme and concentrate on my studies. Fortunately for me, he was busy at the time, so I raced upstairs to the third-floor office of Dean Erland. He was a kind old gentleman who smiled at everyone as he walked across the campus, but who had very little official power. He couldn't see any reason why I should not be allowed to put my play on in the Chapel, so he granted his permission.

I next checked with Mr. Houk, the chairman of the music department, to make sure I wasn't interfering with any scheduled concerts. It was he who dropped the big bombshell on me. We could use the stage for three weeks only. The last week of February was booked for a rehearsal for a concert. My play would have to go on the same nights as the play in the theatre. Oh, well, nothing like a little healthy competition.

I hurriedly gathered up my cast. Made up mostly of freshmen, it included Panda and Bucko. This was fortunate; Panda had decided to go into acting for a career. He had lost over twenty pounds and looked reasonably thin for as fat as he was. I had cast him in the lead role and was confident he would do a good job. Pemby and Stork made up the entire crew, and Mike was chosen to be the light man.

The rest of the cast was a small, motley group of students, most of whom had acted previously. It was essential that they knew how to learn lines quickly, due to the fact that we only had three weeks to rehearse. Following a short pep talk, I sent them away with copies of their scripts and a rehearsal schedule. I sighed in mock contentment as they left, turned to Mike sitting beside me, and said, "Well, there's no backing out now, my friend. It's on with the show."

Theatre Guy made trouble for us early. In a fit, he went to Le Grand Charles and wanted to know how come he had been refused permission to use the Chapel only to learn later that some senior had walked in and received instant approval for his project. My friends in the theatre told me that Le Grand Charles had assured Guy that this was all a big mistake. No one was using the Chapel. I vowed to stay clear of the theatre. I secretly swore that I would obtain all essential materials from some other source, even if I had to steal them. The "if" clause would become a necessary evil.

In the history of theatre there has probably never been so bizarre a three-week period of gathering together the necessary props and set pieces plus promoting the play as well. In the dead of night, my stealthy crew snuck out to obtain the basic furniture for the apartment scene in the play. Mike, Panda, Bucko, Pemby, Stork, and I plodded through the knee-high snow down the long, steep incline. We were about to steal the furniture from the music practice house. Mike, a music major, had assured me they wouldn't mind.

As the six of us entered the near-deserted house to the sound of a piano solo coming from the upper floor, I kept asking myself: if they didn't mind, how come we were swooping down like a band of renegades to carry sofas and chairs away with us? I looked over at Panda's face. He had been experimenting with makeup, but it looked more like war paint to me. The white men thought all the tribes were content on the reservation.

While struggling down the stairs with the couch, we were interrupted by a shocked young girl. For one brief second, I was caught up in the excitement of the evening, the thrill of the theft. I stared coldly into the girl's astonished eyes and said, "Forget everything you have seen here tonight. Go back into that room, close the door, and continue playing your piano. Don't stop until you're sure we are gone."

The now-terrified girl took one look at Pemby, who was holding the couch with one hand and pointing at the open door with the other, and fled into the room.

Snow began to fall over the Hilltop. Six tired boys carried a sofa, two chairs, and a lamp up the steep, white hillside toward the welcoming lights of the Chapel. It was a peaceful, quiet evening. The only sound that could be heard was the melody of the lone piano coming from the music practice house. Poor girl. She was probably found playing the following day with bloody fingers worn down to the bone and eyes transfixed in a wide, horrified stare.

The furniture looked good on stage. Mike had a long talk with Mr. Houk, explaining our borrowing technique and requesting permission to use the materials. Mr. Houk approved of neither, but since the proverbial horse had already left the barn, he saw no reason to shut the barn door on us and gave his reluctant consent.

I wasn't satisfied. I needed a rug for the set. I shuddered whenever I let the very thought of using the Chapel rug cross my warped mind. The Chapel rug. The words were spoken reverently under one's breath. It was rolled out with such pomp only on rare and special occasions, such as when famous orchestras came to play. Ravi Shankar once sat cross-legged on the rug as his fingers danced along the strings of his sitar. To use that same greenish-blue carpet for anything less would be heresy. To use it for a normal student play would be blasphemy. To use it for my play would be certain death; namely, mine.

Flaunting my success with the furniture, I decided to use it. It became a permanent fixture from the moment it was first rolled out for a last week rehearsal. Unfortunately, no one was concerned about its safety.

"All right. There's your notes for the night. Any questions? Good, that wraps it up."

Panda walked right up to me. "Ah, Sean, I spilled some grape juice on the rug. What should I use to clean it up with?"

"What? Where?"

The purple stain might have been blood from my own heart. We spent half the night on hands and knees doing test commercials for various spot removers until it was obliterated to my satisfaction.

The week before the show was hectic enough with lines, lights, last-minute props, and the formerly famous rug. The grapevine sent a message that Le Grand Charles wished to see me. This was <u>not</u> good news.

I publicized the play with flyers and posters before I was called to his office. I decided to have FREE admission for two reasons. Number one was the theatre, which charged one dollar for students and an extra fifty cents for adults. Number two stemmed from a belief that theatre should be treated equally with athletic contests and various concerts. Free is free, no questions asked.

I explained all this before the stern face of Le Grand Charles.

"Please, sir, we've slaved all this time to make it a success. I'm not charging anyone to witness the show. It's free. And people will enjoy it. I got permission to use the Chapel from Dean Erland. Otherwise, it would never have become a reality."

I told him everything. I even unthinkingly offered him a free ticket to the show. For political reasons, I neglected to mention the grape juice stain on the Chapel rug. There was no sense in making enemies in high places.

He paused after my wild outburst. A smile spread slowly across his face.

"Relax," he said calmly. "No one's going to kick you out of the Chapel. It sounds like a good play. I just wanted to make sure you understood all the Chapel rules. Absolutely no smoking. We don't want any smoldering cigarette butts lying around the place. You can understand that, can't you?"

So that was all. Instantly relieved, I assured him no one smoked, bid him a good day, and hurried off to tell half the cast to knock off the smoking.

All the problems and anxieties were worth the final result. The show played to over a hundred people a night, a good turnout for a small school. It even got good reviews from all my friends who came to see it.

My favorite critique came from Miss Maire of the English department. This tall, kindly old woman strode quickly toward me as I made my way up the stairwell. Grabbing my hand and shaking it, she claimed the play was "good, clean fun . . . the best one she had seen in years. Well done, Sean."

I love that great old lady.

Chapter 17 – Spring Fever and Other Incurable Diseases

Aches, pains, illness, bruises, broken bones? The last few months saw an epidemic of sickness and injuries run through our group. The misfortunes drove us one by one into the waiting arms of Doc Mallard. And his various treatments, or lack of them, drove us back out into the street to suffer.

Doc Mallard was very aptly named. He was a quack. The stories about all campus doctors are legendary, but more often than not they are fanciful half-truths based on hearsay. Old Doc Mallard was another story, however. He had built a legend from a bizarre series of unbelievable case histories. In almost every instance, the patient was either mistreated or neglected and had to obtain help from another source. At best, he was a well-meaning individual who constantly made gross errors in medical judgement. At worst, he received his certificate from a box of Cracker Jacks.

There were two things the Doc was most famous for: not X-raying patients, and prescribing "sugar pill" drugs. In the former category, the most preposterous story centered around "Blue Moon" Odonhi, one of the Hilltop's star football players. A shoulder injury in practice forced him to visit the good doctor. Never one to overtax the X-ray machine, Doc Mallard pronounced "Blue Moon" well enough to play in that Saturday's upcoming game. "Blue Moon" questioned the Doc's decision, mainly because he couldn't raise his arm above his waist, went home for a few days, and visited his family physician. The operation on his shoulder was a success, and he was once again able to play football, following a month of rehab.

Knowing about such incidents did not deter Don and Dennis from visiting Doc Mallard after a particularly rowdy basketball game. Don limped into his office. I immediately accompanied Don to Cedar Rapids after the Doc did not X-ray. His foot was broken. Dennis wasn't X-rayed for three days for a "sprained" finger, which also turned out to be broken. When finally set, the finger healed crooked, and appears disjointed to this day.

Although he didn't believe in X-rays, Doc Mallard did have his own cure-all, Sip and Rinse. This mouthwash was a powdery crap in a packet which, when mixed with water, was to be gargled three times a day. It didn't even say on the packet that it helped soothe sore throat pain. But that didn't stop Doc. He prescribed it for colds, fevers, headaches, and stomach viruses as well as throat infections. He even gave some to a head concussion victim once.

Time and time again Doc Mallard struck. While Don hobbled around on crutches and Dennis nursed his broken finger, other friends were forced to call on Doc for his diagnosis. Paul hurt himself lifting boxes and went to the infirmary to check on a possible hernia. Standing nearly naked on a short stool, Paul shifted nervously back and forth while Doc Mallard examined his groin area. Suddenly, without warning, the Doc grabbed his testicles and squeezed tightly. As Paul clutched frantically at the air and turned a light shade of green, the Doc calmly asked, "Does this hurt?"

Yet another time, our old pal Arnie Elston, who graduated early and was in his first year of med school, was visiting for the weekend. The first night with us, Arnie began to suffer from dizzy spells as well as a burning sensation during urination. Don, who had only days before walked again without the aid of crutches, helped me guide our friend across campus at a slow, sometimes unsteady pace. On wobbly knees, Arnie staggered down the long stairway as we balanced his shifting weight on either side. At the infirmary door, we rang the night emergency buzzer. Mrs. Pratt, the night nurse, let us in. After we explained the symptoms to her, she called Doc Mallard at his home.

"Now, what did you say was troubling you along with the dizziness?" she asked Arnie.

Arnie, the pre-med student, replied, "A sharp, burning pain whenever I urinate."

She said, "He says it hurts when he goes to the bathroom."

I'm surprised she didn't ask him if urinate meant number one or number two.

"All right. Thank you, Doctor."

After hanging up the phone, she turned to face us. At least we'd know what Arnie's problem was and what to do to ease his suffering.

"Doctor Mallard says he doesn't know what it is, but if it happens again, be sure to come back and see him."

Great. What a professional diagnosis. If Arnie's still sick tomorrow, I thought, we can come back and get some Sip and Rinse.

Early in April, I came down with one of those never-seems-to-end colds. I sauntered over to the infirmary when the cold moved into my head, and my throat became so sore I could no longer swallow. Doc Mallard probed carelessly around in my mouth with a sterile popsicle stick.

"Oh," he said, "I see you've had your tonsils removed."

"No, I haven't."

Moving right along, Doc Mallard said, "Well, you're running a slight fever, and you definitely have a sore throat, but it's nothing to worry about. You've got the same thing hundreds of kids your age get this time every year. It's spring fever. In a couple of weeks, when the sun shines all the time, and you can chase a few girls and play a little baseball, you'll feel good as new."

"Thanks. Do you have any Sip and Rinse?"

****

The bright yellow and sharp greens of spring were in evidence. The end was in sight. Every walk across campus shook some hidden memory and forced a forgotten smile across my face again. The sun buzzed brightly in the sky every day that last May, contrasting sharply with the two weeks of cold rain that had greeted us four years earlier.

Mike Smith spent the stretch drive on crutches. He had received a minor fracture of his left foot. Mike had forsaken a trip to see Doc Mallard and had gone to visit a reputable doctor in Cedar Rapids, who had fitted him with a walking cast plus crutches. By the time the last week of school rolled around, everyone was used to watching him limp and tired of hearing him complain. May 18 was his twenty-second birthday. His girlfriend had baked him a chocolate cake, which we all knew about. Unfortunately, he was ready to crab his way to some cake during the lunch line.

"I want a piece of cake. I'm damned tired of limping around all day. So, if I want a piece of chocolate cake, then I'm going to have one," Mike growled.

"C'mon, you really don't want one. You've got a lot piled up on your plate," I said.

"What's the matter with you guys?" Mike snatched the piece of cake.

It was only later that he realized his mistake. "You all eat chocolate cake. I'll eat crow."

The last week was hot. It was hotter than all the other hot weeks combined. I took my last final exam on a Thursday afternoon that saw the temperature soar to ninety-eight degrees. My exam grade wasn't about to be that high. I struggled through the last pages of the test and left the old English building. I walked aimlessly across campus, my mind a maze of scattered thoughts. The burning sun shot fiery rays that beat down with a fierce intensity, exhausting me completely.

That same night, we had the senior picnic, an affair meant to be a last informal get-together for our class. We had had a freshmen picnic four years before and then, like now, we were the only group on campus. After eating, Mike, who had shed his cast but not his crutches, joined me in a boys' adventure. We hit fly balls in the middle of the varsity football field.

We had a rubber-coated baseball, one that exploded off the bat and sailed sometimes as much as a hundred yards through the hot, muggy evening. Mike swatted the seams off the ball with each successive contact, and considering he was hitting off a damaged left foot, I was duly impressed every time I had to chase the ball an extra fifty yards.

After an hour of running around sweating, we retreated from the summer heat, the mosquitoes, the honey bees, and headed back toward civilization - in other words, to the Corner for a final beer together.

We moved at a snail's pace up the long, winding sidewalk that led past Gordon Hall, the Chapel, the Administration building, and the Chem building. As we neared the Chapel, we noticed the huge wooden risers that had been recently set up to accommodate our outdoor graduation exercises scheduled for Sunday at noon. The crippled Mike was tired from straining against his crutches, so we stopped to rest on the wooden platforms.

It was as tranquil a setting as anyone would ever see, and I knew we were lucky to be there. The sun's dying beams cast long shadows across the green expanse of hillside spotted with small patches of clover. Towering above us was the white stone structure highlighted by stained-glass windows; beautiful in its gigantic splendor, it had stood for nearly a hundred years. The heat of the day was slowly burning out, leaving in its wake a still, muggy atmosphere.

"Man, it's hot," Mike said, breaking the silence.

"Sure is," I said.

"These lousy crutches slow me down," he said, giving them a fling onto the grass, which stirred up a sudden flurry of activity among the bees.

"Take it easy, will ya? I didn't notice they stopped you from hitting the ball a while ago. You'll be able to take the final march Sunday without 'em."

"Yea," he said pensively. "Boy, Sunday. That soon. Can you believe we'll be getting our diplomas right up here on Sunday?"

"It's hard to imagine," I said, suddenly saddened by the thought. "But, you gotta move on. I mean, you can't stay in one place forever. Still, I'm really going to miss the Hilltop."

"Me, too," echoed Mike. "Where else do you get four years to grow and change but college? Pay the 'Man' at the beginning of the year, and your only responsibilities are making sure you get some papers turned in every week or two." He paused. "Seriously, what are you going to miss?"

"Oh, lots of different things, I suspect. The trips to the Corner, having so many girls close by, Sunday afternoons in the dorm watching the football games, and all of us eating dinner every night."

"And we'll miss our favorite meal, too."

This was the familiar cue for the recitation of the FSOA special. In unison, the two of us chanted, "What's for dinner? Oh, the special, eh? Buffalo balls, French fries, corn, and pink ice cream."

We laughed together, Mike's laugh cutting through the still air. He planned to go into the Air Force in the fall. I knew I would miss that laugh.

"What did you learn all these years, Sean? Do you think it was worth it? You think we can handle the real world outside the womb here?"

"Questions, questions, my boy," I joked. "You're graduating this Sunday. You're supposed to know all the answers."

"I'm a music major, remember? I'm only supposed to know all the notes."

"Well, you know," I said, suddenly serious, "I don't think you can measure what we've learned on paper. My strengths and weaknesses are clearer to me now than they were four years ago. That's when I thought I had only strengths. I've made some good friends, too. Friends for life. That's a rare and precious gift to be taking away from here."

"I think it's better than anything else."

"Did you see the new poster on your ex-roomie's wall? Paul put it up after spring break. It says, 'You never really leave a place. You always take a part of it away with you and leave a part of yourself behind.' That's how I feel about the Hilltop."

"How true," said Mike. "You remember those first weeks? Everybody getting to know each other?"

"Sure do," I chuckled. "Nobody got along."

"Paul used to call you the pain-in-the-ass Cubs' fan."

"Well, it was time he learned there are other cities in the country besides the 'Big St. Louie.'"

"He still hasn't learned that," Mike laughed.

"Remember all the crazy football games? How about that one sophomore year in the pouring rain? We must have been nuts! We were soaking wet!"

"No doubt about it," Mike said. "Did you forget about the time we played tackle football in the snow? We were soaked and cold that time. That'd be fun to do again someday."

"Probably never will though," I said wistfully. "Think about it. We'll all be in different parts of the country, making a living, settling down, miles from each other. Football in the snow? Ha, forget it. That'll just be a memory, one of the days of our youth. But, we won't forget all those memories. Not even old age will drive them all out. And some golden day, when we're sixty-five, we'll burst out laughing or maybe just smile on a crowded street somewhere, and nobody around us will know why."

"Suppose you're right," said Mike. "You ready for that beer yet?"

"Anytime. Let's go get it."

We walked slowly down the hillside toward town as the sun sank. Mike slung his crutches over his shoulder about halfway down.

"I knew all along you were faking it," I said.

Chapter 18 – For Services Rendered

Graduation day. There was a famous popular song (sung by the Four Freshmen) written about it. People for ages hailed its coming. It was always the last day. It marked the completion of a task, the end of an era. Ours was Sunday, May 21, 1972, with ceremonies to begin at noon on the lawn in front of the Chapel. There we would receive our diplomas, our own paper plaques signifying a job well done.

It was a cooler day than we had become accustomed to; the temperature was only in the low nineties. So, if it wasn't cool, it felt that way. The parents had arrived the day before and had attended the open house in the presidential palace on top of the hill. During our visit, I mused on other trips here. Actually, it was the first time I had been inside the house. I had only been to President Skank's mansion twice, when we had sung pumpkin carols at his door on Halloween, and when hundreds of students had slept on his front lawn in protest of the Vietnam War – as if he had manufactured the bombs in his kitchen or something.

After our journey through the Victorian wonderland, we had a fabulous steak dinner in the Union, causing most of the students to wonder where this particular cut of beef had been kept hidden all year. It had been a fun evening for all, what with the edible food and a sudden shortage of four-letter words commonly used by college students but withheld for the sake of innocent parents.

Sunday morning saw the bright sun break over the horizon. There was a breakfast for parents and students at 9:00 and, much like the dinner the night before, it was exceptional. After we gorged ourselves on bacon, eggs, and fresh fruit, my family and I loaded most of my possessions into the car in preparation for the trip home.

Don, Paul, Mike, and I posed for pictures in front of Nilo Hall. (Dennis wasn't there. He ended up two credits short for graduation.) The clicking of the camera along with the black robe and square cardboard hat was about to drive me mad. The four of us stood baking in our sweat-box robes as our parents gleefully snapped picture after picture. After the ordeal, we headed to the spot on the far side of campus where the graduation line would form.

"Arrange yourselves alphabetically," bellowed Mrs. Tucker, who worked in the Administration building. "Check the person in front of you and the one behind you, and we'll come by to make sure you did it right."

She would have made a great kindergarten teacher, I thought. She talked to us like it was nap time, and we better make sure we got the correct rug off the shelf, or we wouldn't get any juice and crackers.

I still couldn't believe this was happening. Another hour and it would all be over. I thought back to the time four years before when we had all walked down this same sidewalk from Gordon Hall to the President's Reception. I was just a scared, stupid freshman then. Now I was a scared, stupid senior, and for just about the same reasons. Something new and exciting was waiting for me from this day on, and there was no rational way to avoid it.

The Chapel bell rang twelve times. The black ants moved quickly toward the delirious crowd. Marching past the adults caused a flurry of motion as more snapshots were taken. Kodak was making a mint that day. If we had been indoors with flashbulbs, I would have been blinded forever.

Sitting alphabetically, I was right next to Paul Mathews. He broke me up more than once, but never more than when he leaned over to me and said, "Shit. Shit. Shit. Our seats are in the sun."

Well, Paul was right. As the ceremony went on, I was about to faint from heat exhaustion. The black robes were not only ugly, they were impractical. Rather than reflecting the sun's rays, they put out the welcome mat, inviting them in to roast our bodies like stuffed ducklings. Even nuns wore white habits in the summertime.

I sat and watched all my friends become instant stars, stealing the limelight for themselves, only to be whisked into obscurity by the next name on the roster. I was watching a parade of people I had watched for four years, and I knew I would only see a handful of them after they stepped off the platform.

I listened carefully to a few special friends' names so I could share in their excitement. "Donald Mark Johnson." Don and I had roomed together for three years, and we had some more years ahead of us. I knew he was destined to be a fine lawyer some day; it was a dream he had held since his early youth. But I still couldn't figure out how someone who loved Thomas Jefferson as much as he did could be such a staunch Republican.

"Paul Spencer Mathews." Paul would remain at the Hilltop as one of the school's top student recruiters. It was the perfect job for someone with a big mouth, and he definitely fit the bill. Future homecomings would be fun for him, but not quite as thrilling.

"Sean Patrick McKay." There it was. I sauntered casually across the stage, shaking hands and accepting congratulations cordially. I was happy. I wasn't even embarrassed that my father was halfway up on stage taking pictures. Smile, wave – click. Thank you, Dad. Click. I almost shook his hand as I bounced down the steps and headed back to my seat.

"Michael Francis Smith." It was off into the wild blue yonder for this future pilot and career man. I couldn't think of a less likely Air Force candidate, but I knew he would be successful. He had a knack for it.

It was over. Everyone broke ranks as soon as the line had moved a short distance. From that moment on, madness prevailed. There was hugging and kissing and promises to write that would be broken before they had a chance to be kept. Good-byes were said that would have to last forever. It was a time of sadness and happiness so uniquely wrapped into one moment that it was impossible to distinguish the emotions from one another. My family and I moved away from the crowd and headed back to the dorm where our car was parked. Halfway across campus, Mike came running toward us, a grin on his face.

"Had to catch you before you got away," he said, panting to catch his breath. "My family's packed and ready to go. I just wanted you to have this before you left."

He handed me a rolled-up scroll, which was obviously a poster. I held it momentarily and then snapped off the rubber band and unfurled it. It was the beautiful poster which had hung in Mike's room, a picture of a chapel on top of a hill with brightly colored trees and stars surrounding it.

"Mike, I can't accept this," I said.

"You have to," he said. "It's a gift. I know you love it. And, besides, you'll probably appreciate it more than I ever would. You can hang it on your wall at the Big U. Where can I hang it? In the cockpit of my plane?"

"Well, thanks." I paused and looked him over. "It's good to see you running again. Take care of yourself, and we'll see you again sometime."

"Stop by and visit us whenever you're in the Chicago area," my dad added. "You're always welcome at our home."

"Will do," said Mike. He ran off after a final good-bye. I knew I was lucky. I had made quite a few good friends on the Hilltop, and that was worth the whole stay.

We piled into the family car. My dad started driving slowly through the small groups of people. He began to turn right out into the street.

"Hold it, Dad," I said. "Do me a favor, will ya? Drive up through the campus just one more time."

The big Buick cruised past the familiar trees and buildings. I waved and yelled out the window at some friends. The car nose-dived down the last long hill. I smiled a contented smile. I was satisfied. There was nothing left to do or say. The memories were mine; everything else would have to remain behind.

As we sped home, I turned around and looked out the back window. The last object I saw was the Chapel, the symbol of this small college. Suddenly, the car dipped down in the winding road, and the Chapel was gone from sight.

Review Requested:
If you loved this book, would you please provide a review at
Amazon.com?
Thank You